THE
TWISTED
WINDOW

THE
TWISTED
WINDOW

Lois Duncan

DELACORTE PRESS/NEW YORK

Published by
Delacorte Press
1 Dag Hammarskjold Plaza
New York, New York 10017

Manufactured in the United States of America

First printing

Library of Congress Cataloging in Publication Data

Duncan, Lois [date of birth]
   The twisted window.

   Summary: Tracy, a high school junior, becomes embroiled in the
problems of a strange boy, who asks her assistance in "snatching" his
half-sister from her father who has allegedly kidnapped her.
   [1. Emotional problems—Fiction.   2. Kidnapping—
Fiction.   3. Mystery and detective stories]   I. Title.
PZ7.D9117Tw   1987   [Fic]   86-29054
ISBN 0-385-29566-9

For my son-in-law
Kenneth David Mahrer

THE
TWISTED
WINDOW

Chapter 1

For over ten minutes now, Tracy Lloyd had been watching the boy with the curly hair watching *her.*

At first she had told herself that she was imagining it. He was not really looking at her, he was looking *past* her, gazing over her shoulder at someone seated at the table behind her. Or perhaps he was looking at Gina. That would not have been surprising. When Gina went braless under one of her collection of tight-fitting mesh tops, male eyes did usually turn in her direction.

But Gina was sitting with her back to the boy. Noteworthy as she might be when viewed straight on, there was nothing so remarkable about Gina's back that a stranger would want to spend his entire lunch period inspecting her shoulder blades.

No, it wasn't Gina who had attracted his attention.

Tracy lowered her eyes to her plate as though concentrating on her half eaten sandwich.

"The new guy," she said, "you know, the one we were talking about earlier? The one who was standing by the water fountain when we were getting our books this morning. He's sitting two tables over, and he keeps staring at us."

"Mr. Gorgeous?" Gina enjoyed pegging people with

private nicknames. "Don't you *wish* he really were. Don't *I* wish it! He looks like that guy who had a 'face that launched a thousand ships.'"

"That wasn't a guy," said Tracy. "It was Helen of Troy. And I mean it. He really does seem to be looking us over."

"And here I sit, facing the wrong way. Mr. Gorgeous has his eyes glued to this table, and I'm missing this incredible chance to chalk up Brownie points. Life can be so cruel!" Gina paused, considered a moment, and then said, "I'm going to drop my fork, okay? Then I'm going to bend down and get it and straighten up slowly. *Very* slowly. And then I'll raise my eyes—also very slowly—and let our gazes meet. Sparks will fly, I guarantee it. Is he still looking over here?"

"Yes," Tracy told her. "In fact, now he's getting up from his seat. He's picking up his plate."

The boy was moving with obvious deliberation. There was no doubt at all about what he was planning to do.

"You're not going to believe this," Tracy said quietly to Gina, "but your Mr. Gorgeous is on his way over to sit with us."

That was the one, Brad told himself. That was the girl. She looked just as right to him now as she had that morning. She had the look he was after—attractive, but not a bit flashy—a look that made him feel comfortable and at ease. She was dressed in a tailored blouse with a high collar, and her dark hair was pulled back from her face in a clean and simple style that contrasted sharply with the wild blond mane of the girl she was sitting with.

He had spotted her yesterday afternoon, just after the last bell had rung, but at that time the main thrust of his attention had been directed toward somebody else. The girl he had been considering then had been on the plump side, and the excess weight had made it hard to determine her age. As he had been preparing to go over and strike up a conversation, however, a boy had materialized out of nowhere, thrown an arm around the girl's shoulders, and whisked her away.

That, of course, had been the end of that. The girl was out of the running. He needed a loner, not somebody equipped with a boyfriend.

A slender dark-haired girl had been standing three lockers down from the plump one, and with the loss of the one, Brad's eyes had been drawn to the other. He had been struck by an immediate feeling of recognition, as though he already knew her from somewhere else. Although she looked nothing like the girl he had previously been considering, she might be equally good for the purpose he had in mind. She was tall and pretty, with an air of subtle aloofness that made her appear more mature than the average high school student. If the quality of her voice was in keeping with her appearance, she might easily be able to pass herself off as old enough to have her own apartment.

The girl had finished stuffing her books into her locker, shoved the door shut, and clicked the padlock into place. Then she had turned and made her way down the crowded hallway. At one point, a boy in a plaid shirt and cowboy boots had attempted to intercept her, but she had put him off with a polite nod and impersonal smile. At the end of the hallway she had exited the building, still alone and apparently intending to continue that way.

That had been the last that Brad had seen of her yesterday, but he had thought about her a lot and had even awakened once in the night with a picture in his mind of the girl and Mindy together. Drugged with sleep, he had not been sure if he was experiencing a dream or a vision, but he had been pleased to see that the girl's hand had been resting protectively on Mindy's shoulder.

This morning he had gotten to school early and had entered the building as soon as the janitor had unlocked the doors. Once inside, he had stationed himself by the watercooler across from the girl's locker. Soon after the first bell rang, a busty girl with hair too blond to be natural had rushed up to the locker and started twirling the combination lock. Several minutes later the girl for whom he had been waiting had joined her there, and the two of them stood together, chatting casually, as they hauled books and gym clothes out of the locker and sorted through them.

The blonde was a nonstop talker. Her mouth was in constant motion, and she kept tossing her head, to cause the bleached hair to swirl around her shoulders, and glancing about her to see if she was being noticed.

At one point her eyes had zeroed in on Brad, and she had thrown him a cute, come-on smile.

He had stepped away from the fountain, hurriedly averting his eyes.

Sorry, blondie, he had told her silently. I bet you're one hot little number, but you are definitely not what I'm shopping for.

When the second bell rang he had gone to the library and waited out the morning there, and then at noon he went to the cafeteria and bought himself lunch. It had been a wasted half hour, for the girl had not put in an appearance. In order to avoid having to socialize with the students seated around him, Brad read while he ate. He had no interest in striking up a conversation with anyone other than the girl, and he knew that the fewer people he talked to, the safer he would be.

When the cafeteria began to empty out, Brad scraped what was left on his plate into the garbage bin, placed his tray on the pile by the door to the kitchen, and drifted back out into the hall. He killed some time washing and rewashing his hands in the boys' room, and then, when the bell rang to signal the start of B lunch, he reentered the cafeteria as part of a new stream of hungry students. He went through the line again and paid for the second tray of food, hoping that the woman at the cash register would not recognize him. To his relief, she showed no sign of it, plucking the money from his hand and dropping it into the drawer of the register without glancing at his face.

He chose a table by the wall where he could sit and have a full view of the room. The problem was that students were entering through two different doors, and it was difficult to keep watch on both simultaneously. He loaded his fork with spaghetti and took a token bite, trying to fake an appetite. It would be just his luck, he thought, for the girl to be scheduled for C lunch, which would mean that he would have to eat yet another time. Worse still, since Winfield High School had an open campus, it was possible that she might have gone off to eat at some fast-food restaurant, in which case she would never show up at the cafeteria.

B lunch was nearly over when he suddenly saw her sitting at a table only two away from his own. He could only imagine that he had been looking at the wrong door when she had made her entrance, for she had evidently already been through the line. She was seated on the far side of the table, facing in his direction, while her companion, the sexy blonde with whom she shared a locker, was seated opposite, with her back to him.

Brad laid down his fork and cemented his eyes on the dark-haired girl's face. Once again, he was struck by how familiar she looked. Several moments passed without her appearing to notice that he was watching her. Then the force of his concentration seemed to penetrate her consciousness. Her own eyes lifted to meet his, held his gaze a moment, and then flickered nervously away. Her friend was jabbering, jabbering, jabbering, and she was pretending to be absorbed in the chatter, but he could tell by the self-conscious way she was nibbling at her sandwich that she was only half listening. She sneaked another quick glance in his direction and looked hurriedly away again.

Brad got to his feet, picked up his tray, and walked over to the table where the two girls sat. His girl—he was already identifying her in his mind as "his girl"—spoke hastily to alert her companion, who swiveled around in her seat to watch him approach.

"Hi," Brad said. "I'm new at this school, but I've already gotten the word that this is the table where all the action takes place. Is it just a rumor, or did I get the right story?"

"Don't we wish!" the blond girl said pertly. "Don't we really wish! If there's any action in Winfield, it's a well-kept secret."

"Then maybe we need to stir some up," Brad told her, flashing the smile that his best friend, Jamie, had always jokingly referred to as "the golden grin that can charm birds out of the trees."

"Do you mind if I sit down?" Brad asked. "It's hard to generate action when you're holding a tray that's dripping spaghetti sauce."

"Be our guest," the blonde said with a giggle. "We could use some company. I'm Gina Scarpelli, and this is Tracy Lloyd."

"Nice to meet you both. I'm Brad Johnson." Brad set his tray down on the table next to Gina's and swung his legs over the bench so he could take his seat beside her, diagonally across from Tracy.

"I've got this talent for reading the vibes people

throw off," he said. "The ones coming off you girls are really strong. I'm getting the message—it's sort of a tingling sensation when I do this trick—that you're the type who might share a locker across from a watercooler."

"Boy, what a talent! How ever do you do it?" Gina gave her head a provocative toss that sent her long hair swinging. "The vibes *I* get about *you* are that you like to hang around water fountains. I saw you there this morning looking us over."

"You did, huh?" Brad said. "Well, it's possible you might be right. When you start a new school, you do have to case things out. It's been my experience that the VIP lockers are usually right across from drinking fountains. That's like a universal law."

"Well, it's a law that doesn't apply in our case," said Tracy. "Gina and I are lowly juniors." Her voice was low pitched and mature-sounding, exactly as he had hoped it would be.

"Where do you come from, Brad?" asked Gina.

"Albuquerque," Brad told her. "My dad's a geologist. He got offered a job here with an oil company. How about the two of you? I bet you're not native Texans. Everybody here seems to come from someplace else."

"Not me," said Gina. "I've never lived anywhere but Winfield. Tracy's a newcomer though. She's from New York City."

"You've got to be kidding!" Brad exclaimed with mock astonishment. "I always thought New York was a place people went *to,* not a place they came *from.*" He directed the "golden grin" at Tracy. "What brought you here? Did your dad get a too-good-to-turn-down job offer, too?"

"My mother died last summer," Tracy told him. "I moved here to live with my aunt and uncle."

"I'm sorry," Brad said. It was not an answer he had anticipated. "I guess I really put my foot in it that time."

"There was no way you could have known." Tracy picked up her sandwich, bit off a corner, and set it back down on her plate.

"It must be hard changing schools so close to the end of the school year," said Gina in an obvious attempt to switch the conversation to a less awkward subject. "What's your schedule, Brad? Maybe we have some of the same classes."

"I don't think so," Brad said. "Most of my classes are—"

The final portion of his statement was drowned out by the sound of the bell signaling the end of B period lunch. There was an immediate rush of activity at adjoining tables as those students who had been engrossed in conversation or trying to beat the clock by bolting down second helpings were jolted to attention.

Tracy and Gina got quickly to their feet, and Brad followed suit, picking up his tray for his second trip to the garbage bin.

"Do you really think the food's that awful?" Tracy asked him, nodding at his plate, which was still piled high with mounds of untouched spaghetti. "Next time, you ought to try a sandwich."

"I don't know about that," said Gina. "I remember one time when there was a flub-up in the kitchen, and they mixed the tuna with mustard instead of mayo. That was pretty gross." She turned back to Brad. "What class are you headed for now?"

"It's . . . it's . . ." He groped hastily for a subject that was required by high schools everywhere. "It's English literature."

"I have English next period too!" Gina exclaimed.

"Do you need to stop at your locker, or shall we head straight over?"

"I may not be taking the same course as you," Brad said. "Are you taking Shakespeare?" When Gina shook her head, it was all he could do to suppress a sigh of relief. "I was taking Shakespeare back in Albuquerque, so they put me in that class here too. It's going to be tough though, because we're not studying the same plays."

"Well, so much for that." Gina made no attempt to conceal her disappointment. "Being new in town and all, if you find yourself getting desperate for human companionship, I'm always good for some friendly conversation. We're the only Scarpellis in the phone book."

"Thanks, I'll keep that in mind," Brad said. He turned to Tracy. "How about you? Are you the only Lloyds in the phone book?"

"My uncle's name isn't Lloyd," said Tracy.

The tone of her voice had changed in some subtle manner, and Brad experienced a chill of sudden apprehension. Had he made some stupid blunder that had given him away? He hurriedly reviewed their conversation but could come up with nothing that should have aroused suspicion. Except for her own disclosure that she had lost her mother, there had been nothing said by any one of them that had been anything other than casual and impersonal.

It was obvious, though, that she was not encouraging him to phone her. Was it possible that she already had a steady boyfriend? In the short time Brad had been observing her, there had been no such indication. On several occasions, in fact, he had seen her cold-shoulder boys who were obviously trying to strike up a conversation with her. Perhaps she was going with somebody who attended another high school or was away at college.

By now the cafeteria had almost emptied out. Both

Tracy and Gina had already deposited their plates and trays in the appropriate receptacles and were headed for the door.

Struggling to hide his disappointment, Brad added his own tray to the pile by the entrance to the kitchen and followed the girls out of the cafeteria into the hall. The corridor was filled with students involved in an attempt to get from one class to another within a five-minute time span, and the reverberating clang of locker doors made normal conversation all but impossible.

With a parting nod and smile, Gina plunged into the river of moving bodies and was promptly swept off in one direction, while Tracy disappeared in another. A wave of students who were headed for C lunch almost bowled Brad over as he fought his way against the current to the center of the hallway.

I'll have to find somebody else, that's all, he told himself. There are plenty of girls at this school who can do the job for me.

But Tracy had seemed so *right,* so exactly what he needed. Time was racing by so quickly. It was Tuesday already. There were only five days left before spring break would be over back in Albuquerque, five days before his mother would report him missing. The prospect of starting over at this point, of finding another appropriate girl, of getting to know her well enough to talk her into helping him, seemed overwhelming.

Then, just as he was trying to psych himself up to plunge back into the search, miraculously there was Tracy, standing in front of him.

"It's Stevenson," she told him, raising her voice so that it would carry over the noise in the hallway. "My uncle and aunt are named Cory and Irene Stevenson."

"They're in the phone book?"

"Yes—it's Stevenson, spelled with a *V.*"

"I'll call you tonight," Brad said. "Will that be okay?"

She hesitated and then nodded, and he was filled with a sudden rush of euphoria.

It was an omen! His plan was destined to work!

Chapter 2

From the first day she had registered at Winfield High School, Tracy had taken the same route home every afternoon—two blocks east along Third Street, one block south on Rosemont, and a diagonal cut across Lamar Park to Cotton Road. Her aunt and uncle's home, at which she still felt more like a visitor than a resident, was located on South Cotton, in a neighborhood of manicured lawns and neatly shaped shrubbery. It was populated primarily by middle-aged working couples, and on weekday afternoons there was an air of emptiness about it, like a movie set on a day when there was no filming.

Except for several weeks last September, when the mid-afternoon sun had been so intense that she had arrived home dizzy with heat and drenched with perspiration, Tracy had never minded the walk to and from school. Since there were few families with teenagers living on South Cotton, there was no one she felt obligated to walk with, and the solitary twenty minutes at either end of the school day had quickly become one of the few real pleasures in her current life. Her aunt, a real estate agent, worked irregular hours, and all too often, Tracy arrived home from school to find Aunt Rene already there waiting for her, eager to visit and "have a nice chat" about the events of the day. Because of this, Tracy usually tried to prolong her walk as much as possible.

Generally she used this time alone for emotional unwinding. Today, however, she had some heavy thinking to do. She had done something on impulse that had not only been stupid but possibly even dangerous, and she did not know why she had done it or what she ought to do next.

She should never have encouraged Brad Johnson to get in touch with her. It had been a crazy thing to do, and at the time she had sensed that. It was not even as if the invitation had come tumbling out in an accidental manner during the course of their lunchtime conversation. She had been even more brazen than Gina, whose line about being "the only Scarpellis in the phone book" was a standing joke at school. Gina, at least, had tried to sound philanthropic—"If you get desperate for human companionship" was the way she had put it. In Tracy's case, there had been no such pretense. She had left the cafeteria and, once she was safely away, had deliberately turned back to hand herself over to a stranger who, even then, she had had good reason to believe was a fraud.

Why had she done such a thing? she asked herself. Was it because of his extreme good looks? Yes, if she were to be honest, she would have to admit that that had certainly been part of it. Although slight in build, the boy who called himself Brad Johnson had a face that was almost too handsome to be believed. The perfect features; the heavy-lashed eyes and the wide, sensitive mouth gave him a look of ethereal beauty that was very different from the burly cloddishness that she had come to associate with the "Winfield rednecks."

When Gina had first pointed him out to her—"Mr. Gorgeous over there by the water fountain is checking us out!"—Tracy had glanced across with no more than idle curiosity and surprised herself with her immediate positive reaction. She had not had the slightest interest in dating since she had arrived in Winfield, but the sight of this particular boy had had a strange effect on her. He looked like the type of young man she was used to seeing at the theaters and museums and art galleries she had attended with her mother. When she had seen him again at noon in the cafeteria, it had been hard to pretend to be listening to Gina's chatter. She had known even before he got up from his seat that he was going to come over to their table, and she had known, too, that she wanted him to do just that.

It was not until later that she had come to realize that he was not what he was pretending to be.

Now, shifting her load of books from one arm to the other, Tracy left the sidewalk and crossed Rosemont Street to the northwest corner of Lamar Park. Rows of trees flanked the park's entrance, and almost as soon as she stepped onto the gravel pathway the afternoon sunlight was blocked by leafy branches, and shade settled onto her shoulders with weighted coolness.

The park was laid out as a rectangle and arbitrarily divided into sections, each of which was unofficially designated for a particular use. The northern end, screened off by a golden wall of forsythia, was a romantic haven for lovers. There, on spring and summer evenings, young people lay entwined in each other's arms like pink and white islands dotting a grass green sea. The center of the park was wide and open and provided an unobstructed area for dog walking, ball playing, or frisbee tossing. The southeast corner, bordering on Cotton Road, was the playground area, and contained swings, slides, and a set of monkey bars. Benches were positioned at strategic points along the edges of the playground so mothers could sit and visit with each other while remaining alert, on call to rescue children who got stuck on the bars or clobbered by swings.

The park was always liveliest in the early mornings. That was when the joggers were out, dressed in bright sweat suits, chugging clockwise around the park's perimeter like center-ring ponies in a circus. The dog walkers were active then, too, clinging to leashes and carrying their pooper scoopers, enthusiastically greeting each other like members of some elite fraternity. When she cut through the park in the mornings on her way to school, Tracy often felt as though she were crashing a private party.

In the afternoons usually only the playground was occupied. Today, as she walked past the beds of pansies beside the fountain, she could see, framed in a gap between two bushes, several young women chatting together at the park's south end, while a group of small children chased each other up and down the slides.

It was then that she suddenly realized that she was being watched.

There was no specific reason for the awareness, but it was as undeniable as the feeling she had experienced at lunchtime when she had felt Brad Johnson staring at her. On that occasion she had been disconcerted yet flattered; there was nothing sinister about being the object of someone's attention in a school cafeteria. What she was feeling now, however, was something quite different, because the person who was watching her was keeping himself hidden.

She was alone in that section of the park—or, at least, she had assumed she was. Tracy glanced surreptitiously about her, hoping to find that she had been mistaken. Even a child, stretched out on the grass behind the fountain, would provide an innocent explanation for what she was feeling.

A hasty perusal confirmed the fact that no such person existed. To all appearances, she *was* alone, as she had thought she was. And yet she felt certain this was not true. Her skin was starting to prickle, and her scalp was getting a tingling sensation, as though an icy wind were blowing against the back of her neck.

The first thought that flashed into her mind was that she was being staked out for a mugging. With effort she fought the temptation to break into a run. If she ran it would alert her pursuer that she was aware of his existence, and the last thing she wanted to do was trigger an attack. She began to walk slightly faster to get away from the trees, the most likely shelter for someone who wanted to conceal himself. She did not permit herself to glance back over her shoulder but kept her ears tuned for the telltale sound of crackling bushes or a sudden burst of footsteps rushing up behind her.

A scream lay formed and ready at the back of her throat. If she released it, the mothers at the playground would be sure to hear her, but the bushes would block their view of what was happening. How they would react to a disembodied scream was hard to anticipate. For all she knew, their whole concern might be for their children. Instead of rushing to her assistance they might grab their youngsters and run the other way.

Never before had the northern end of the park seemed so vast and empty. She was by now well past the fountain, but the hedge of forsythia seemed to stretch on indefinitely, cutting her off from any human contact. She could hear the sound of her own breathing, as ragged and rasping as though she had just run a marathon, and the muscles in her legs were cramping with the effort it was taking her to hold them in check.

Walk, don't run, she counseled herself. Steady and fast will get you there. You've made a lot of progress during the past few minutes. Anybody hiding back behind the trees will have a lot of distance to cover before he can get at you now.

If he was still back behind the trees. *But what if he wasn't?* What if he had left his station there and was closing the distance between them, while the pounding of her heart drowned out his footsteps?

Pull yourself together, Tracy commanded. There isn't any reason to panic. This is a little town in Texas, not New York City. It's the middle of the afternoon, not two in the morning.

Besides, even if she was correct about the fact that someone was observing her, that did not necessarily mean he was out to molest her. No halfway intelligent mugger would risk a daylight attack on a schoolgirl who was obviously good for nothing but an armload of textbooks.

The hedge extended only several more yards before it ended at the edge of the softball field. If she did run now, she told herself, she would be certain to reach the clearing before anyone pursuing her could overtake her.

With that realization, Tracy found her legs taking over for her brain. Without having made a conscious decision to do so, she started to run. Sprinting to the end of the hedgerow, she hurled herself around the last of the bushes and burst out into the open section of the park.

The relief that swept over her drained all strength from her body and left her light-headed and gasping like a half drowned swimmer. The world around her shimmied as though distorted by heat waves, and her legs felt loose-jointed and rubbery.

Then, as moments passed and her heartrate gradually returned to normal, she deliberately turned and peered back at the empty expanse of grass that stretched innocently to the flower-encircled fountain. No one was there, of course. Nobody had been chasing her.

For a fleeting moment she contemplated the possibility that she might also have been wrong about being watched. Then, as if to lay that doubt to rest, she heard a car door slam and an engine start up beyond the trees and shrubbery that blocked her view of Rosemont. It was the first car engine she had been aware of since she had entered the park. Rosemont was a small residential street where there was little traffic, except in the early morning, when its residents left for work, and from five to six o'clock in the evening, when they returned home.

The rumble of the engine leapt to a roar, and a squeal of tires pierced the afternoon quiet like a shriek of pain. Too surprised to react, Tracy stood frozen for an instant too long. By the time she had thought to drop her books and run back along the path to the street, the throb of the motor had already been softened by distance.

He's gone, she thought, disgusted with herself for not having moved quickly enough to have identified the driver. Even so, the sound of the car speeding away in such an unorthodox fashion was proof of sorts that she had not been the victim of paranoia.

What she had sensed had been real—as real as the danger her mother must have sensed in that final incredulous instant before she felt the knife.

Chapter 3

Brad cursed himself all the way from the park to the motel. Following her had been an inexcusably risky thing to have done. It had also been pointless. There had been nothing to be gained by driving along at a snail's pace a block and a half behind Tracy Lloyd as she walked from Winfield High School to her aunt and uncle's home.

It was not as though he had needed to find out where the house was. When they had parted company after B lunch, he had immediately left the school building to locate a public phone booth, where he had looked up the name Cory Stevenson in the directory and found the address listed as 1214 South Cotton Road. When he flipped to the city map in the back of the book he discovered that Cotton was a north-south street, located only about a quarter of a mile to the east of the school.

He had torn the corner off the cover of the phone book, jotted down the information he needed, and stuck the scrap of paper in the pocket of his jeans. Then, with the whole long afternoon still stretching in front of him, he had decided to kill some time by going to the movies. In the dark interior of a nearly empty theater situated in a shopping mall, he shared two hours of an old James Bond flick with three middle-aged women, a whimpering baby, and an elderly drunk who evidently had seen the picture before, because he kept shouting warnings to 007 whenever danger threatened.

Despite the drunk's contagious enthusiasm, once ensconced in the theater Brad found himself unable to concentrate on the picture. He was too souped up, too excited about the way things were going. It was going to work after all—at least, it appeared that way. The fact that Tracy had returned on her own to tell him how to get in touch with her convinced him it was preordained she was to be his partner.

When the movie was over he managed to use up most of another hour walking through the shopping mall. He was not surprised to find many of the same stores that he was used to seeing in New Mexico and felt he was on familiar turf as he strolled past Sears, a Little Professor bookstore, a Hallmark card shop, and a Thom Mc An shoe store.

Midway along the mall's lower level he came upon a sporting goods store with a display of target pistols in the window. He stood for a number of minutes, staring longingly at the handguns laid out behind the glass. How he wished he had one of those instead of the cumbersome hunting rifle that he had brought with him from Albuquerque! He considered going into the store and trying to buy a pistol but decided against it. He was unfamiliar with the Texas laws that governed the purchase of firearms and did not want to risk being asked to present ID.

He left the shopping center at approximately half past three, drove aimlessly about for a while, and then, as if drawn by a magnet, headed back to the high school. Classes had been out for some time now, and the student parking lot was practically empty. Several small groups of teenagers stood chatting beside the few remaining cars, but it was obvious that the brunt of the students had long since taken off for home.

Brad pulled up across the street from the school and hung there with the engine idling, watching a group of younger boys laughing and shoving each other around on the steps of the building. Had there ever been a time when he had been that carefree? As if in answer, a picture flashed into his mind of himself as a ten-year-old, rough-housing with his friend, Jamie, during recess. Taller and stronger than Brad was back in their preteens, it had been Jamie who had taught him to stand up for himself so he wouldn't get picked on. Over the years he'd had some wonderful times with Jamie, but he had never been part of a group the way these boys were.

The kids on the steps eventually began drifting over to the bicycle rack. Brad put the car into gear. There was nothing more he could do until evening, he told himself, so he might as well drive back to the motel and watch some television.

Pulling away from the curb, he shifted into second. That was when he saw her, a little more than half a block ahead of him on the far side of the street. He recognized her instantly, even from the back, by the set of her shoulders and her graceful, long-strided walk. Although he had seen her for the first time only the day before, already she seemed incredibly familiar.

He glanced at his watch and then back at the girl on the sidewalk. It was late for her to be leaving school. He wondered what could have held her there this long. The sight of her at a time when he had not been looking for her made him feel like the recipient of an undeserved present. Without making a conscious decision to follow her, he kept the car in second gear and inched it along, letting the distance widen between them so that if for some reason she turned to look back, she would not notice he was tailing her. She walked two blocks along Third Street and then turned onto Rosemont. When, a few moments later, Brad, too, came opposite the corner, he was startled to find that she had vanished.

Not *vanished,* he corrected himself. Nobody just *vanishes.* Maybe she had entered one of the houses on the west side of the street. That didn't seem reasonable, though, since the Stevensons' address had been listed in the phone book as being on South Cotton. A second possibility occurred to him; perhaps she had crossed the street and gone into the park. A gravel path ran diagonally in from the corner, but a row of trees and a screen of flowering bushes cut off his view of the interior, so he could not tell whether or not she had entered.

Once again, acting strictly on impulse, Brad stopped the car, turned off the motor, and got out. He crossed Rosemont and walked down the path until he came to the inner edge of the clump of trees. Standing in a pocket of shadow formed by the leafy branches, he was surprised at the extent of his relief at seeing Tracy some twenty yards ahead of him.

He struggled against the temptation to call out her name. For a moment he actually contemplated doing so. He had intended a slower approach—first a casual phone call, then perhaps a movie date, and, if those went well, the initiation of an in-depth talk during which he would explain to her what had to be done. Much as he hated the idea of wasting time in such a manner, he had been afraid that if he moved too quickly she might refuse him. He had thought he would start the ball rolling by phoning her that evening. Now he found himself wondering if the elaborate preparation was necessary.

While he was trying to decide whether to take advantage of this unexpected opportunity or to stick with his original, more carefully conceived plan, Tracy broke into a run. The suddenness of her flight took Brad by such surprise that he froze where he was and then moved hastily back into the protective covering of the bushes. What in the world had happened? he asked himself. He was not aware of having made a sound. She had not glanced over her shoulder, so there seemed to be no way she could have known he was there. Somehow, though, she had sensed it, and that realization had been enough to send her skittering away like a frightened rabbit.

Brad silently cursed himself for his own stupidity. How could he have been idiotic enough to have let this happen! Now she was all worked up, and by this evening when he made his phone call, she would probably have developed a full-blown case of the jitters. There was no telling what the result of that might be. She might not even be willing to come to the phone.

The one thing he did know for certain was that it was imperative that he get out of her range of vision before she reached the edge of the hedgerow and decided to turn around to look behind her.

Hurrying back along the path to the street, he quickly got into his car and turned the key in the ignition, cringing as the afternoon quiet was broken by the roar of the engine springing to life. There was no way Tracy could have missed hearing that racket, he thought grimly, and it was bound to reinforce her suspicion that she had been followed. He knew her too slightly to be able to predict her reaction. She might panic further at this indication that someone had indeed been spying on her, or she might throw caution to the winds and rush back to investigate.

Either way, he knew he had to get out of the area. Brad threw the car into gear and clamped his foot down hard on the accelerator, glancing apprehensively into the rearview mirror as he did so. He could see no sign of

Tracy, but that did not necessarily mean that she would not come popping out from behind the trees at any moment.

With that thought in mind, he drove the first few blocks of Rosemont as though it were the Indianapolis Speedway. Then, reminding himself that the last thing he needed was to get arrested, he slowed to comply with the residential speed limit and drove carefully back to the Trade Winds Motel. Parking in his designated space, he got out of the car, fumbled in his pocket for the key, and let himself into unit twenty-three.

The venetian blinds slanted almost closed across the room's one window, and except for the thin lines of sunlight that lay in horizontal streaks along the front edge of the mud-colored carpet, the room was as dark as though it were nighttime. When he left to go to the school that morning, Brad had deliberately left the air conditioner running, but in his absence the maid had evidently come in and turned it off. Despite the fact that it was only April, the air in the unventilated room was so stale and stifling that it was all he could do to force himself to enter.

Locating the light switch by touch, he flicked on the overhead. The room materialized before him—twin beds with mattresses sagging beneath brown quilted spreads, one straight-backed chair, and a chest of drawers that served as a stand for a black and white television set. Dingy beige curtains, which might once have been cream-colored, hung limply at the sides of the window, and the mirror that was mounted on the door leading to the bathroom was smudged with handprints.

When he had driven into Winfield two days earlier, Brad had been tempted to set up residence at the Holiday Inn at the western edge of town, but after pricing it he had decided to find someplace less expensive. Although he had withdrawn the contents of his savings account

manuscript. Also enclosed is a letter of instruction from
er the printout.

ince the printout is black and white, these changes are
at has been added is in boldface type, and any word,
leted has a strike through the center of the space it
gin next to any line that contains a redlined change.

e. The mechanical alterations I've marked have been
eral compliance with the <u>Chicago Manual of Style</u>, 15th
, 11th ed., and Johns Hopkins UP style preferences.

address: missing words (articles, pronouns, and
nny sentences (fixed by an occasional added

prior to making the trip, his car had proved to be a gas guzzler on the open highway, and he would have to feed its fuel tank on the return trip also. In an attempt to pinch pennies, he had ended up at the Trade Winds.

Pushing the door closed behind him, he crossed the room to the air conditioner and turned it on, shoving the thermostat to its lowest setting. His backpack lay open on one of the two beds, displaying a tumbled assortment of T-shirts, socks, and underwear. His father's old hunting rifle stood propped against the wall in the corner of the room.

Aside from the backpack, clothing, and gun, the only thing in the room that was his own was the photograph of Mindy that he had placed on the corner of the bureau. It was an inexpensive K Mart special, in which, clad in a sleeveless yellow sundress, she was incongruously posed in front of a painted backdrop of autumn foliage. The sun-bleached highlights in her pale hair emphasized her smooth midsummer tan, and her eyes were sparkling with laughter, as though the photographer had just finished telling her a marvelous joke.

Brad stood for a moment, staring at the girl in the photograph. She was so lovely it made his heart ache to look at her.

Gavin can't have you, baby, he told her silently. I'm going to get you back. Tracy Lloyd doesn't know it yet, but she's going to find you for me, and when I leave this place, you're going to be with me.

He checked his watch. It was twenty minutes past five. He tried to imagine what Tracy was doing at that moment. Should he phone her now, he wondered, and invite her to go out with him? He could suggest a movie later that evening. After considering for a moment he decided it might be wiser to wait a little while longer before calling her. That would allow her a chance to recover from her fright in the park, and he could use the time to unwind a bit and take a shower.

The bathroom in unit twenty-three was as uninviting as the bedroom. The walls and ceiling of the shower stall were speckled with mildew, and the water that emerged from the corroded shower head pattered on Brad's shoulders in an ineffectual drizzle. After spending what seemed an eternity trying to rinse soap scum from his body, he gave up the battle, dried himself off with a sour-smelling towel, and returned to the bedroom, where he stretched out on the bed to watch a rerun of *M*A*S*H*. He had no intention of falling asleep and was startled when he suddenly realized that the scenes flickering in front of his just opened eyes were from a *National Geographic* documentary.

This time when he glanced at his watch he caught his breath in horror and snapped into a sitting position so quickly that his stomach muscles went into a spasm. *Eight o'clock!* Two full hours had passed since he lay down. There was no way that he could call a girl at this hour and ask her for a date for the very same evening. His only chance now of getting to see Tracy Lloyd would be to turn up on her doorstep and hope for the best.

Chapter 4

Tracy was not surprised to hear the doorbell ring at twenty minutes past eight. It was as though, subconsciously, she had been waiting for it all evening. While dutifully consuming the corned beef her aunt had served for dinner, while rinsing the plates and silverware and loading the dishwasher, while working a page of algebra problems and scanning a chapter in her world history book, her ears had been tuned for the sound of the door-bell or telephone.

"I'll get it!" she called now to her aunt and uncle, who had taken root in the living room an hour earlier for their usual marathon round of postdinner television watching.

She went out into the entrance hall and opened the door. As she had expected, Brad Johnson was standing there.

"Hi," he said. "I've been told this is the house where all the action is. I thought I'd better come by and check out the rumor."

"I think I've heard that line somewhere before," said Tracy.

"You're right," Brad acknowledged easily. "It worked so well at lunch today I thought I'd try it again." He smiled at her. "Want to go get a hamburger at McDonald's?"

"Thanks, but I've already eaten," Tracy told him. "Hours ago, in fact. My aunt serves dinner right on the dot of six."

"Then maybe you've had enough time to get hungry again," Brad said. "If not, come along for the ride and to keep me company. Order a Coke or something. Take pity on a lonely newcomer. After all, you're the only person I know in Winfield."

"You know Gina," Tracy reminded him.

"If I'd wanted to buy Gina a hamburger, I would have called her. I do know she's 'the only Scarpelli in the phone book.'" His smile broadened, as though the two of them were sharing a private joke. "I'm afraid Gina's not my type."

"And you think I am?"

"I think you might be. I'd like a chance to find out."

"Has it occurred to you that you might not be *my* type?" Tracy's voice was cool, and she did not return the smile.

"I don't get it," Brad said, looking puzzled. "You said I could call you. I thought that meant you wouldn't mind going out with me."

"Tracy?" Aunt Rene called from the adjoining room. "If that's the boy collecting for the paper, tell him I mailed his check yesterday."

"It's not the paperboy," Tracy called back to her. "It's somebody from school."

"Then invite her in. There's no sense holding a long conversation in the doorway."

There was a moment of silence, during which Tracy could picture her plump aunt struggling to hoist herself out of the easy chair that was her designated evening nesting place. Then, the feat having been accomplished, she came bustling out into the entrance hall.

"Why, hello!" she exclaimed, obviously surprised to

discover her niece's caller was a boy. "I'm Mrs. Stevenson, Tracy's aunt."

"Nice to meet you," Brad responded politely. "I'm Brad Johnson. I stopped by to see if I could talk Tracy into going out for a Coke."

"That doesn't seem such a good idea on a school night," said Aunt Rene. "Young people need their sleep if they're going to be alert in class."

"But it's only eight thirty!" Tracy protested. "You can't expect me to go to bed at that hour!"

"This close to the end of the school year, you must have homework," her aunt said. "Finals are coming up soon. Shouldn't you be studying?"

"I've finished my homework, and we don't have finals for a month yet." Tracy knew even as she spoke that what she was doing was ridiculous. Her aunt had provided her with the excuse she needed, and she should have been taking advantage of it. It would be nothing short of lunacy to go out alone with this stranger who, she had come to suspect, might not even be named Brad Johnson.

Despite that, she heard herself speaking up defiantly. "Actually, a Coke would taste pretty good right now. That meat we had for dinner tonight made me thirsty."

"Tracy, dear, I really don't know about this," said Aunt Rene. "Maybe we ought to see what Uncle Cory thinks."

Tracy turned to face her aunt, disconcerted as always by the distorted resemblance to her mother. Even after seven months of living in the Stevensons' home, she still had not become fully adjusted to seeing Danielle Lloyd's small, neat features and expressive eyes in the alien setting of Irene Stevenson's fleshy face.

"We're going to get a Coke," Tracy stated firmly. "We won't be long. We're just going over to McDonald's."

Without giving her aunt a chance to voice further

objections, she stepped through the open doorway into the sweet spring evening.

"I'll have her home in an hour, Mrs. Stevenson," said Brad.

"Well, see that you do." Aunt Rene regarded them helplessly. "Have her back by nine thirty at the latest, and be sure to drive carefully!"

Brad's light blue Chevrolet Impala was parked in front of the house. He started to lead the way to it and then slowed his pace when he realized Tracy was not following along behind him.

"Is something the matter?" he asked, turning back to face her.

"I want to walk," Tracy said.

"Walk?" Brad stared at her in disbelief. "You want to *walk* all the way to McDonald's over on Eighth Street?"

"We don't need to go to McDonald's," Tracy told him. "I don't really want a Coke. I only said that to get the point across to Aunt Rene that I'm sick to death of her salty corned beef." She spoke slowly and carefully in an attempt to conceal her nervousness. "What I'm trying to say is, I don't want to ride in your car."

The smile slowly faded from Brad's face.

"What's wrong with my car? You have something against Impalas?"

"No," said Tracy. "I don't have anything against the car itself. The thing is, I don't ride with people I don't trust."

She started to walk north along the sidewalk in the direction of Third Street. After a moment's hesitation, Brad took a few swift strides and fell into step beside her.

"I don't get it," he said in bewilderment. "I thought we were friends."

"Let's not play games, Brad—if your name actually *is* Brad," Tracy said. "If you're looking for someone gullible, then Gina's your better bet. She believed everything you told us in the cafeteria. She's a small-town girl who doesn't know much about con men."

"You're talking crazy," Brad said.

"No, I'm talking smart. I let myself get snowed at lunch today, but that isn't going to happen again." She glanced across at him in an attempt to read his expression, but as they passed beneath a streetlight his eyes were thrown into pockets of darkness. "You were lying when you told Gina you were taking Shakespeare. I took that class myself last semester. I had to take it then, because it isn't offered in the spring."

"You're right," Brad said after a moment's hesitation. "I did lie about that."

"That's not all you lied about," Tracy continued. "The truth of it is you're not even a student at Winfield. I stopped by the office after school today and asked the secretary to look up your name. There isn't any Brad Johnson in the computer register. The secretary told me this same sort of thing has happened before. Last spring there were a couple of young guys who kept hanging around the campus, acting like they were students. It turned out they were dealing drugs they'd smuggled up from Mexico."

"I'm not pushing drugs," Brad said.

"Then what *are* you pushing?"

"I'm not pushing anything. It's not like that at all." They had come opposite the park now, and he gestured toward a bench positioned in the shadows at the edge of the playground. "Let's go over there and sit down. It's too hard to talk when we're walking."

"I'm not going into the park at night," said Tracy. "Just this afternoon, right in broad daylight—" She broke off in mid sentence, struck by what she was saying. A wave of comprehension swept over her, and she swung abruptly around to confront him. "It was *you*, wasn't it? *You're* the one who was hiding and spying on me!"

"I did follow you into the park today," Brad admitted. "I don't see anything so terrible about that. I needed to talk to you and wanted to catch you alone. I didn't expect you to go tearing off like you did before I'd even had a chance to call out to you. Come on over and sit down and I'll tell you everything."

"You can explain anything you need to explain right here."

"What are you scared of?" Brad asked her jokingly. "Do you think I'm Jack the Ripper, looking for a victim?" When Tracy didn't respond, he regarded her incredulously. "Seriously, is that what you do think? Don't tell me you're afraid I'm going to attack you!"

"That sort of thing does happen," Tracy told him. "It happened to my mother. Mother was an actress with a walk-on part in a Broadway show. She was just getting home from work one night when she was robbed and stabbed. It happened in the hall right outside our apartment."

Brad seemed taken aback.

"That's heavy," he said. "It's no wonder you're jittery about strangers. Still, that didn't have anything to do with me. I give you my word, I don't go around stabbing people."

"Why should I trust you when I don't even know who you are?"

"My name's Bradley Johnson," Brad said. "If you want proof, I can show you my driver's license. I come from Albuquerque, just the way I told you at lunch."

"At lunch you also told me you were a student at the high school."

"I had to say that, or you wouldn't have been willing to talk to me. There's something important I have to get done in Winfield. I went to the school to see if I could find someone to help me."

"And I lucked out and got chosen?" Tracy's voice was edged with sarcasm. "So, when do you plan to tell me what my duties are?"

"I have to locate a girl," Brad said, ignoring the tone of the question. "Her name is Mindy, and I think she may be in Winfield."

"I don't know any girl named Mindy," Tracy told him.

"I didn't expect you would, but you can help me find her."

"Why do you need to find her? Did she run away?"

"Hardly," Brad said shortly. "Do you want to see her picture?" Without waiting for an answer, he fished in a pocket of his shirt and extracted a color photograph. He thrust it out at her. "That's Mindy, the way she looked last summer."

Tracy glanced at the picture, casually at first, and then with more interest. "Why, she's only a baby! I thought you were talking about a girlfriend."

"She was eighteen months old when Mom had this picture taken. Like I said, that was back last summer. By now, she's two and a half."

"Your *mother* had this picture taken? Mindy's a relative?"

"She's my sister," said Brad. "No, actually, she's my half sister. My father died of a heart attack on my thirteenth birthday. Then my mother married a guy named Gavin Brummer. They had Mindy, and not too long after that, Mom and Gavin got divorced."

"You don't look much alike," said Tracy. "Mindy's so blond."

"She gets that from Gavin. My dad had brown curly hair." He paused, as though trying to decide how to phrase his next statement. "Four months ago Mindy was taken."

"Taken?" exclaimed Tracy. "Do you mean she was *kidnapped?*"

"That's the term I'd use," said Brad. "The cops call it 'child-snatching.' Gavin had been hanging around our place all that morning. He finally got me so mad I couldn't take it any longer, and I drove over to my friend Jamie's house to simmer down. Mom thought Gavin was leaving when I was. He was out in the yard, saying good-bye to Mindy, when our phone started ringing inside the house. Mom went in to answer it, and when she came back out a few minutes later both Gavin and Mindy were gone."

"Does your mother have custody of Mindy?" Tracy asked him.

"Of course Mom has custody. Gavin's a creep."

"My mother got custody of me when my folks were divorced," Tracy said.

Brad was too caught up in his own story to respond to the statement.

"Mom fell apart after Mindy was snatched," he said. "So did I, for a while there. I guess you could say we were both in shock. You get so used to trusting people in authority, and Mom and I sat back like a couple of zombies, waiting for the police to track Gavin down."

"I shouldn't have thought that would have been hard," said Tracy. "From things I've read, it seems like it's almost impossible for people to disappear without a trace. They take pieces of their old lives with them when they relocate. They look for the same kind of work and stay in touch with relatives. Gavin wasn't a stranger, he was your stepfather. You must have some idea about how to find him."

"I do," said Brad, "but the police weren't interested in hearing it. Lieutenant Souter, the officer in charge of the investigation, treated me like I was a moron, too young or too dumb to say anything worth listening to. Mom was just as bad. She wouldn't listen to me either. I tried to get her to hire a private detective, but she couldn't seem to take in what I was suggesting.

"That's when I decided to do my own detective work. I called the office where Gavin had worked and asked if they had any idea where he might have gone. His boss wouldn't talk to me, but the boss's secretary did. She told me Gavin had written for a job recommendation. She couldn't remember the town the letter came from, but she did recall it was in Texas. When she said that, it suddenly hit me that Gavin had gotten a birthday card a few months earlier from a sister in Winfield. Like you said, people who 'disappear' tend to keep in touch with relatives. It seemed to me that Winfield would be a good place to look for him."

"That makes sense," Tracy acknowledged. "But even if he's moved here, wouldn't it be likely he'd be going by another name?"

"I thought about that," said Brad, "but I decided I'd check it out anyway. I called directory assistance and what do you know, they have a new listing for a G. Brummer at the Continental Arms."

"How did the police react when you told them?" asked Tracy.

"They wouldn't *let* me tell them," Brad said bitterly. "When I tried, Lieutenant Souter said I ought to see a shrink. Mom wouldn't give me a chance to tell her either. She started crying and said, 'Stop this crazy scheming. Can't you just accept the fact that your sister is gone?' "

"It sounds like your mother's the one who needs a shrink," said Tracy. "Doesn't she *want* her daughter found?"

"Mom's not exactly with it right now," said Brad.

"After Mindy was taken, she had a sort of a breakdown. It's not the first one she's had. She's a fragile sort of person. She's never been able to handle stress very well."

He lapsed into silence, and the sounds of the April evening rose to fill the void: the wail of a baby fighting sleep in a crib by an open window, the voice of a mother calling a child to come in for his bath, the drone of a radio providing mood music for an unseen couple in the park across the street.

After a moment, Tracy said, "I bet he didn't take your sister because he loved her. I bet he only wanted her so your mother couldn't have her."

"You're right about that," said Brad. "How did you know?"

"I've been through it myself," Tracy told him. "When my own folks got divorced, my father made a big production about wanting custody. Dad's an actor, a lot better known than my mother was. The case was written up in all the Hollywood tabloids—'Richard Lloyd Devastated by Loss of Daughter.' After Mother was killed, though, he pulled a total about-face. He decided he didn't want me with him in Los Angeles. Instead, he sent me here to live with Mother's sister and her husband."

"I'm sure that's how it must be now with Gavin," said Brad. "I checked out the Continental Arms the day I got to Winfield. It's a singles apartment complex that doesn't allow children. If he *is* living there, he's got to be keeping Mindy stashed away in a back bedroom or something so the people who run the place don't know he's got her."

"*If* he's living there?" Tracy repeated. "You mean you're not certain? I thought you said you'd been over there to investigate."

"I got as far as the entrance hall," Brad told her. "One of the mailboxes, number two oh four, is marked Brummer-Tyler. There's no way to tell by that whether Brummer is Gavin. If it *is*, I can't run the risk of having him see me. I need to have somebody else case out the apartment and find out for sure what the situation is."

"Then that's why you came to the school today."

It was a statement, but Brad responded to it as though it were a question. "Yes, I went to your school to try to find someone to help me." It was his turn, now, to strain to make out the expression on a face half lost in shadows. "Will you help me, Tracy? Please?"

I don't want to get involved in this, thought Tracy. I don't want my life touched by anybody else's. I don't want to care about Mindy, I don't want to care about Brad—I don't want to invest myself in anyone again.

Considering the situation, though, she knew she had no alternative.

"What exactly do you want me to do?" she asked.

Chapter 5

When she entered the house, Tracy was greeted by the nasal twang of a television newswoman raised in dramatic recitation of the day's events. She shoved the door closed behind her and started across to the stairs.

"Tracy?" her aunt's voice called from the living room. "Is that you?"

"Yes," Tracy responded. "I'm going upstairs to bed."

"Tracy, will you come in here, please?"

It was her uncle's voice this time.

Turning back from the stairs, Tracy recrossed the hall to the doorway leading into the living room. Her aunt and uncle were seated in twin easy chairs in identical positions in front of the television set, looking like Tweedledum and Tweedledee in *Through the Looking-Glass*.

"What is it, Uncle Cory?" she asked.

"Your aunt has been worried about you," said her uncle. "You told her you'd be back by nine thirty. In case you haven't noticed, this is the ten o'clock news we're watching."

"I'm sorry," said Tracy. "Brad and I got talking and lost track of time."

"That's not a good enough excuse," said her uncle. "When you make us a promise, we expect you to keep it.

We've taken on the responsibility for raising you. You're going to have to respect that and live by the rules of our home."

"I'm sorry," Tracy repeated. "It won't happen again. If it's all right with you, I'm going to go upstairs now. It's a school night, and Aunt Rene wants me alert in class."

Turning away from the doorway, she went back into the hall and ascended the stairway to the second floor. At the top of the stairs she turned and went down the hallway, past the blue and lavender master bedroom, past the bathroom, with its lilac deodorizer fumes, past a second small bedroom, which her aunt used as her home office, and stopped at the last door on the right.

She opened it and reached in to flick on the overhead light. The room that leapt into being was as fluffy and flowered as though it had sprung full-blown from the pages of *Seventeen*. Until the previous September, it had served her aunt and uncle as a combination guest and storage room, but when it had been decided that Tracy would be coming to live with them Aunt Rene had hurriedly redecorated it in a style she thought more appropriate for a teenage girl. When she had spent her first night there, Tracy, whose walls at home had been plastered with Picasso reproductions and whose bed had been covered with an Indian tapestry, had felt as though she was masquerading as Little Bo Peep.

Tonight, however, she did not notice the frills and flounces. Stepping into the room, she closed the door and locked it and went over to the window facing out onto South Cotton Road. The glow of the streetlight in front of the house illuminated the street, and she could see that Brad's Chevy was no longer parked by the curb.

I don't ride with people I don't trust, she had said that evening. She had not trusted him then, and she was not sure she did now. Even so, she had promised to help him locate his sister. She did not know why, but it was something she felt compelled to do.

The lighted windows of the house across the street stared out from beneath their half lowered blinds like heavy-lidded owl eyes. A breeze stirred the filmy curtains at the sides of the window, and the oak tree in the Stevensons' front yard rustled softly, as though its leaves were whispering secrets to each other. A renegade branch scraped the roof with a rasping sound, like fingernails searching for a clawhold on the rainspout.

Tracy stepped back from the window and pulled down the blind. A lamp with a rose-colored shade stood on the table next to the bed. She switched it on and turned off the glaring overhead. In the gentler light, the room's assorted shades of pink became suddenly softer, the various patterns blending in a way they had not done previously.

She took her pajamas out of the top drawer of the bureau and put them on. Then she went over to the neatly made bed and turned back the spread, exposing pink flowered sheets.

Her mother would have referred to those sheets as "cutesy-poo."

"Your aunt has always been one for cutesy-poo things," she had commented once upon receiving the Stevensons' Christmas card, which portrayed a fluffy kitten tangled up in ribbon from a gift-wrapped package. "When we were children, Rene was the type who had the days of the week embroidered on her panties."

Danielle Lloyd had borne no resemblance to her sister.

Even back in Tracy's own childhood, when her parents had still been together, both struggling unknowns trying to break into show business, her mother had lived in a world that was simple and elegant. Stark white walls and curtainless windows. A single rose in a crystal wine-glass. Wool slacks, tailored to her slender, long-legged figure. A handbag purchased at a secondhand store but made of quality leather.

During the custody battle her father's attorney had made an issue of the fact that his client would be able to provide his daughter with a privileged childhood.

"With her father, Tracy would be able to live graciously," he had said.

"I live graciously, too," Tracy's mother had countered. "Not as expensively, I'll grant you, but just as graciously. I don't care how successful Richard may have become, there is no way I will ever give up my daughter."

There is no way I will ever give up my daughter!

Her mother had spoken those words with such determination, yet now, only three years later, she was gone from Tracy's life. In an instant's time in a dimly lit hallway at two in the morning, while she struggled to fit her key into the lock of their Brooklyn Heights apartment, Danielle Lloyd had been robbed of her chance to see her daughter grow up.

Mother! Tracy cried silently. Oh, Mother, *I miss you!* She mouthed the words in the way one might offer up a prayer.

Ironically, as though in response, there was a tap on the door. "Tracy?" Aunt Rene's voice called softly. "You aren't asleep yet, are you?"

"No," Tracy said to the closed door. "I'm not asleep yet." She did not say, come in.

Despite the lack of any welcome, she could hear her aunt attempting to turn the knob. It was a moment before she seemed to take in the fact that the door was locked.

There was a short silence. Then the voice on the other side of the door said, "Tracy, I really wish you wouldn't do this. If there was a fire, you could be trapped in there."

Tracy went over and turned the knob, releasing the lock. She pulled the door partially open.

"Okay," she said. "Let the fires rage; there's no danger now. What can I do for you, Aunt Rene?"

The woman who stood in the hallway regarded her with grave concern.

"I just wanted to explain about tonight," she said. "Uncle Cory didn't mean to speak so harshly to you, dear. We're both happy to know that you're beginning to make some friends here. We want you to do all the normal things young girls do—join clubs, baby-sit, go to parties and out on dates. It's just that we feel so terribly responsible. With your dear mother gone and your father so far away—"

"I know," said Tracy. "It's okay."

"Not having had children of our own, this is all so new for us. We want so much to do everything the way we ought to. Your father did entrust you to our care, and if anything ever were to happen to you, we couldn't live with ourselves."

"It's okay," Tracy said again. "If you don't mind, Aunt Rene, I'm awfully sleepy. Could we talk about this another time?"

"Yes, of course," her aunt said. "Of course. You must go to bed now. I'm glad you had a nice time tonight. Your friend, Brad—he seemed very nice, so well-mannered and attractive. He really does have the most beautiful eyes and smile. Perhaps you could invite him over on the weekend. We could rent a nice movie to play on the VCR." She leaned forward and brushed her lips across her niece's cheek. "Sleep tight, dear, and don't let the bedbugs bite."

"I won't," said Tracy, trying not to flinch at the cliché. "Good night, Aunt Rene."

She closed the door and stood waiting until her aunt's receding footsteps had run their course down the length of the hallway. Then she relocked the door and got into bed.

She switched off the bedside lamp and the room dissolved into darkness. When she closed her eyes, she could feel the weight of the blackness pressing down upon her eyelids and boring its way into her soul. The room was so heavy with silence that she could hear the thud of her own heartbeat. Even after all these months, she still had not become accustomed to the absence of sound in adjoining apartments and the lack of traffic noise in the street beneath her window.

She thought of the little girl in the yellow sundress and of the child's mother, immobilized by loss. She tried to visualize the father, the horrendous "child-snatcher." Even his name had an evil ring to it, like the stage name of an actor who played villains. When she pictured Gavin Brummer, what she saw was a vision of her father, back when she herself had been the age Mindy was now.

Brad was right; the man must be found and the child brought home.

He doesn't love her, thought Tracy. It's all just a game. A man like that has no room in his life for a child. He doesn't deserve a daughter, and he shouldn't have one.

The fact that she had not met him was insignificant. She did not need to meet Gavin Brummer to hate him. She knew all she needed to know about turncoat fathers, having acquired that knowledge from Richard Lloyd.

In unit twenty-three of the Trade Winds Motel, Brad lay awake also, staring into the darkness and trying to still the turmoil in his mind. When he did at last doze off he slept fitfully and lightly, caught in a semiconscious state of mental turbulence that fluctuated between rational thought and disoriented dreaming. Shortly before daybreak, he either thought or dreamed he heard Jamie speaking words that had been uttered two weeks before. "It's not going to work," Jamie said. "You don't know what you're doing. Even if you do locate Gavin, it won't do any good."

"Then you aren't coming with me?" asked Brad, his heart sinking.

"No, I'm not," Jamie said. "You mustn't go either. No matter how hard you try, you won't get your sister back. Tracking down Gavin would be a terrible mistake."

"You're the one who's making a terrible mistake," Brad said. "I *am* going to find Mindy, no matter what you and Mom say. I was counting on you to help me, but if you won't, then I'll just have to look for somebody who *will.*"

He awoke to the sound of his voice mumbling groggily, "find somebody who *will,*" and opened his eyes to find the dull gray light of dawn seeping through the thin slits between the venetian blinds.

He lay for a time without moving, staring up at the ceiling, reviewing both Jamie's statement and his own. He still could hardly believe his friend had fallen down on him. The two of them had always supported each other in everything.

In the end he had lied to Jamie, as he had to his mother. He had told them both he was going to spend spring break up at his father's old cabin in the Pecos Mountains.

His mother had been upset at the thought of being left alone for a week. "You know how I hate being all by myself," she had said piteously.

"I've got to make sure the place survived the winter

all right," Brad had told her. "There was a lot of snow this year, and it might have caused some damage. That cabin adds a lot to the value of the property. We want it to be in good shape when the time comes to sell it."

Now, hundreds of miles away from the fresh green beauty of the Pecos Wilderness, he lay in a lumpy bed in a third-rate motel in Texas, reliving the previous evening and making plans for the day ahead. Watching the room grow slowly lighter, he tried not to listen to the sound of the Trade Winds coming to life on either side of him. Through the thin wall there came the rush of a toilet being flushed in an adjoining bathroom. Then pipes started to rattle as somebody turned on a shower. The doors of the various units began to open and slam closed, and a car engine sputtered to life outside Brad's window.

He made no move to get out of bed and participate in the morning activity. He knew there was nothing more he could accomplish on his own, and Tracy would not be available until school let out.

How ironic, he thought, that a stranger would listen and believe him, when the people he should have been able to count on had failed him. Well, he didn't need any of them now—not his mother, not fair-weather Jamie, not Lieutenant Souter. Now that he had Tracy, he would not be alone anymore.

Brad drew a long breath and willed himself to relax. There was nothing to be gained by rehashing his problems.

Rolling onto his stomach, he pressed his face into a soft hollow in the lumpy pillow and sank at last into the solid state of oblivion that had eluded him throughout his restless night.

Chapter 6

The Continental Arms was a four-sided apartment complex laid out in a rectangular design, with all the units facing out upon the landscaped, open-air recreational area at its center. The building could be entered in one of two ways, either through an underground garage or through a street-level set of double security doors. The first of the security doors led into an entrance hall, which contained a row of mailboxes labeled with the names of tenants. Visitors were required to buzz an occupant and identify themselves over an intercom. The tenant could then, if he or she chose, press a button that would release the lock on the inner door and allow the visitor entrance.

Brad had investigated the situation upon his arrival in Winfield and had come to the conclusion that the better way of gaining entrance to the building was through the underground parking area.

"The tenants activate the garage door with remote control boxes," he explained to Tracy. "Once the door rises, they're usually too set on getting their cars inside to notice much else. That's especially true during rush hour, right after people get off from work. It's a madhouse then."

Now, standing with him across the street from the

apartment house, Tracy had to agree that his observation had been correct. It was 5:45 in the evening, when the surge of homecoming traffic was at its peak, and the garage door was lifting and falling like a battery-powered guillotine. Even so, she regarded the situation with measured doubt.

"I can't make myself invisible. Even with all the chaos, *somebody's* bound to see me."

"The driver of the car behind you will, but he won't be able to do anything about it," said Brad. "He won't have a chance to react before the door cuts him off." He paused and then asked, "You're not getting cold feet, are you?"

Tracy shook her head. "I don't want to make any mistakes, that's all."

"You won't. After all, you're the daughter of professional actors. You can pull it off. All you have to do is find out if this Brummer is Gavin." He put his hand on her arm and gave it a reassuring squeeze. "I'd go into the building with you, but I'm afraid to risk it. If Gavin ever once caught sight of me, the game would be over. He'd take off with Mindy, and all we'd see would be dust. I promise you, though, getting in there is going to be easy."

This did, indeed, prove to be the case. When the door reached the peak of its next ascent, Tracy was able to step quickly into the garage on the tail of a cream-colored Subaru and slip unchallenged into a shadowy passageway between two rows of parked vehicles. By the time the door had fallen and risen again, she was well on her way to the elevator at the corner of the basement.

She rode up to ground level in the company of two men in business suits and a woman in a nurse's uniform. Then, stepping out into the spaciousness of the recreational area, she found herself greeted by pink-tinged twilight, the astringent odor of chlorine, and planters filled with an array of flowers and shrubbery.

It was immediately apparent that the area around the pool was a regular gathering place for the more social-minded residents of the Continental Arms. Despite the fact that it was still early, the after-work crowd had begun to congregate, and the patio had already developed a partylike atmosphere. Several people were splashing in the pool, and at least a dozen others were either sitting on the edge or relaxing in deck chairs with glasses and beer cans in hand. There was a lot of talk and laughter, and a portable tape player was spewing forth rock music as background for conversation.

Tracy stood for a moment, absorbing the scene before her. Was it possible that one of these men was Brad's former stepfather? If so, she thought, he must be much younger than Brad's mother. This attractive group of people appeared to be in their twenties and early thirties, and men and women alike were as uniformly healthy and trim as though their bodies had been cloned at a Nautilus fitness center.

Shifting her attention to the apartments themselves, Tracy noted that the units at ground level were identified by three digit numbers starting with the numeral one. Stairways at either end of the recreation area led to the second level of the building, where the higher-numbered apartments faced out upon a walkway overlooking the pool.

The nearest set of stairs was situated next to the elevator she had ridden up on. Leaving the pool party churning behind her, Tracy mounted the steps and walked slowly along the balcony, counting off the numbers of the apartments until she stood in front of 204. A card inserted in a slot next to the buzzer read BRUMMER–TYLER.

I don't have to do this, she reminded herself. I don't

owe a thing to Brad Johnson. I can still change my mind
and turn around and walk out of here.

She pressed the buzzer.

She could hear the sound of it, faint and far, at the
back of the apartment. For several moments there was no
additional sound from within. Then, just as she was preparing to accept the fact that no one was going to answer,
the door was yanked open to reveal a shirtless young man
with a towel thrown across his shoulders. He was barefoot,
and his matted hair was glistening with droplets of water.
With the hand with which he was not grasping the doorknob, he was cinching the belt of a pair of Levi's 501s.

He did not seem disconcerted to find his caller a
stranger.

"Hello, there," he said in cordial greeting. "Sorry for
the delay, but you caught me in the shower. If I'd had any
idea somebody this gorgeous was standing at the door, I'd
have come racing out in a bath towel."

"If you'd like me to wait until you've finished—"
Tracy began haltingly, thrown off balance by such an en-
thusiastic welcome.

"Not at all. I'm decent now, and if it will make you
feel more comfortable, I'll even put on a shirt and shoes in
your honor. Why don't you start by telling me who you
are? After that, you can come in and give me the story of
your life."

"My name's Tracy Lloyd," said Tracy. "I'm a new
neighbor of yours. I just wanted to ask if it would be
possible for me to use your phone."

"No problem about that. Beautiful ladies are always
welcome here. I'm Jim Tyler." The man thrust out a
damp, freckled hand for Tracy to shake. "I was certain I
hadn't seen you around here before. Did you just move
in?"

"This morning," Tracy told him. "I haven't had time

yet to get a phone installed. In fact, the call I need to make is to the telephone company."

"Be my guest." Jim Tyler stepped back from the doorway and motioned her in.

She stepped past him into the living room and glanced about her, half expecting to find a blond child curled up on the sofa. Instead, she saw a pile of newspapers and a copy of *TV Guide*. The room was furnished in an impersonal manner that revealed almost nothing about the apartment's occupants. The abstract prints on the walls matched the shades of rust in the two-tone carpet, and the couch, chairs, and coffee table might have been purchased as a set during a sale at Sears.

To Tracy, the apartment appeared on first glance to be less a real home than a short-term stopover area in which swinging bachelors could change their clothes between social engagements. She could see nothing anywhere to indicate the presence of a child.

"This is nice," she commented politely. "I have a single myself. I'd been wondering what the double apartments were like."

"The only real difference is that the living room's bigger," said Jim. "Then, of course, there's an extra bedroom and bath." He gestured toward the door to the kitchen. "The phone's on the wall to the left of the sink, and unless my roommate's dragged it off somewhere, the directory ought to be on the counter."

"Thanks," Tracy said. "I shouldn't be more than a minute."

When she entered the kitchen, she found that it, too, had the look of a room that received sporadic use only. The remnants of breakfast—a cup half filled with cold coffee, an apple core, two cereal bowls with milk scum dried on their interiors—still sat out on the table. An orange juice carton stood on the counter, and the sink was speckled with charred fragments of blackened toast. The dishwasher gaped open, the bottom section empty and the top shelf stacked with cups and glasses. A trash container standing next to the refrigerator was filled with cartons from frozen dinners topped off by a heavy sprinkling of empty beer cans.

Despite the extent of its clutter, there was nothing about the room to proclaim the fact that one of that morning's breakfasters had been a child. No high chair stood in the corner adjacent to the table; no food-spattered bib hung draped across the towel rack. There were no parental reminders attached with magnets to the refrigerator— *Pick up Mindy's sitter at five. Take Mindy for allergy shot. Parent Open House at Mindy's nursery on Friday.*

Jim Tyler had not accompanied her into the kitchen, but, conscious of the open doorway, Tracy picked up the telephone directory and riffled through its pages as though busily engaged in looking up a number. Then she lifted the receiver and held it to her ear.

"Hello," she said against the buzz of the dial tone. "I'd like to see about getting a phone installed in my new apartment. My name's Tracy Lloyd, and I'm at the Continental Arms." She paused, as if listening to someone on the other end of the line. "That's right," she continued, "it's Lloyd, spelled with two *L*s. . . . No, I've never had a phone in my own name before." Another pause to listen to the nonexistent second party. "Thank you. I'll be there tomorrow, then. Good-bye."

As she was replacing the receiver, Jim appeared in the doorway. His hair, though still damp, was no longer dripping, and he was wearing a T-shirt and sandals.

"So, what's the good word?" he asked. "When can they install it?"

"Next week, I hope," said Tracy. "I have to go down to their office and sign some papers."

"Hassles!" Jim said lightly. "The whole world's filled with hassles!" He opened the door of the refrigerator. "What can I offer you in the way of refreshments? Beer? Pop? How about a rum and Coke? A bunch of us took a run down to Mexico last weekend and brought back some duty-free Ronrico."

"A Coke would be great. Nothing in it, please," said Tracy. She moved to stand beside him so she, too, could peer into the refrigerator. She was not sure what it was she hoped to find there—bowls of Jell-O, perhaps, or a container of Kool-Aid. Maybe even a Donald Duck glass filled with chocolate milk. All she saw were beverage cans, some apples, and a wedge of cheese.

Jim extracted a Coke and a beer, handed the former to Tracy, and shut the refrigerator door. Then he led the way out of the kitchen. Shoving aside the newspapers that littered the sofa, he sat down, motioning Tracy to take a seat beside him.

"Well, tell me about yourself," he said. "You can't be from around here; you don't have the mandatory drawl. I'd guess you're from somewhere in the East. Am I right?"

"I'm from New York," Tracy told him. Then, anticipating the next question, she continued, "I moved here to be near my family—my aunt and uncle. They're sort of elderly and not too well."

For some reason she found that statement difficult to utter. She was surprised by that fact, for the overall deception did not bother her. As Brad had noted, she was the product of a theater background, and playing a role came naturally and easily to her. Still, the lie about the Stevensons made her oddly uncomfortable. She wished she could have thought fast enough to have come up with some other reason for having made the move from New York to Texas.

"Have you been able to find a job yet?" asked Jim.

This was another question for which she had not prepared herself. Where would it be logical for her to say she worked? Although she might appear mature enough to be out of high school, she knew she did not look old enough to be a college graduate. What sort of job could she reasonably be expected to hold that would permit her to afford an apartment at the Continental Arms?

She was taking too long to answer.

Jim regarded her strangely.

"Don't tell me," he said. "Let me guess. I think you're a spy."

"A—spy?" Tracy echoed.

Then she saw the twinkle in his eyes and realized he was teasing her.

"Don't try to deny it. You've been hired by Ewing Oil. Your mission is to check out the oil fields around Winfield and let J.R. know which ones to buy into."

"How did you guess?" Tracy asked with a nervous laugh.

"I was trained by the CIA," Jim said, laughing with her. "All joking aside, though, what is it that you *really* do for a—"

The question was cut off by the jangle of the telephone.

"Oh, no!" Jim exclaimed in mock exasperation. "Please, excuse me while I answer that. It's probably the White House calling again. The President just won't take no for an answer, and I do find his parties so boring."

He got up from the sofa and went out to the kitchen. The phone broke off in mid shriek, and Tracy heard Jim saying, "Hello? Oh, hi, Debbie, how are you doing, pretty lady?" There was a pause. "You got tickets for *that?* I thought they were all sold out! Hey, I'd love to go, but I'm going to be out of town this weekend. I've got a couple of days of vacation coming, and I'm taking off in the morning for Padre Island. You might give my roommate a try though. He's really bummed out. That's one guy who could use a little R and R."

Grateful for the timely interruption, Tracy seized the opportunity to turn her attention to the hall leading back to the bedrooms. Although there had been no sign of a child's presence in either the living room or kitchen, if Mindy did indeed reside in this apartment, there was bound to be some evidence in the room she slept in.

Moving quietly, Tracy got to her feet and hurriedly crossed the living room to the hall. Of the three doors that opened onto the hallway, two stood ajar. The first of these led into a bathroom still misted with steam from Jim's shower. Nothing there indicated a child's recent presence; no potty-chair sat next to the toilet, no toy boats or rubber ducks lined the edge of the tub.

Jim's voice drifted out from the kitchen.

"He's having dinner at his sister's tonight, so you can probably catch him there. Hey, wait a minute, I just remembered something. It's possible he may not be available either. He was telling me this morning that Friday is Doug and Sally's anniversary. I know they've been having a hard time finding sitters. If they're planning a big night out, he might be stuck with the kid."

The second open door led into a bedroom. This, too, appeared to be the sole province of an adult. The bedside table was piled with copies of *Playboy,* and a huge black and white poster of a well-endowed young woman in an infinitesimal bikini hung on the wall above the headboard. The bed was unmade, and a shirt with a tie still wound around the collar lay tossed across it. A pair of water skis was propped in a corner of the room, and the handle of a tennis racket protruded from beneath the bed.

Tracy stepped back from the entrance to the bedroom and turned to face the closed door directly opposite. Did she dare take a chance and open that? From what she could overhear of his conversation, it did not seem probable that Jim would remain on the phone much longer. "I don't have the number," he was saying, "but they're listed in the phone book. The last name's Carver. If you call tonight, maybe there'll still be enough time for them to dig up a sitter."

I've come this far, thought Tracy. I can't stop now.

She gave the knob a twist and shoved the door open. Disappointment surged through her as she saw that, although it was neater, this second bedroom bore no more resemblance to a nursery than the first room had. There was no sign of a youth bed or crib, nor were there toys. No dolls or crayons or picture books lay scattered about.

Entering quickly, Tracy crossed to the closet and pulled open the sliding door. She was confronted with an array of men's clothing—shirts, trousers, a rack of neckties. There were no tiny blouses and overalls, no little dresses. She glanced down at the floor. The shoes that were lined up there were obviously those of an adult— one black pair, one brown pair, some well-worn Nikes, and a pair of thongs.

Brad had to be wrong, she thought. Wrong, or maybe even crazy. Was the story he had told her true, or had he invented it? Did he really have a sister who had been kidnapped? Was there truly a wicked stepfather named Gavin Brummer? If so, then perhaps it was nothing more than coincidence that Jim Tyler's roommate had the same last name and first initial. The one thing of which she had now become absolutely certain was that no child lived in the Brummer-Tyler apartment.

Sliding the closet door closed again, she turned and started back across the room to the hall.

She had taken only three steps when suddenly she saw it.

In a silver frame on the table next to the bed, there stood a photograph of a blond baby in a yellow sundress.

Chapter 7

The Douglas Carver residence was listed in the phone directory as being on Sweetwater Drive, a street in a middle-class housing development on the eastern outskirts of Winfield. It was an odd, winding street that seemed to exist for the sole purpose of avoiding contact with any main artery of traffic, and by the time Brad had finally managed to locate it and follow its snakelike route to the twenty-seven hundred block, night had fully descended and turned the houses on either side of the street into faceless black rectangles.

"That's twenty-seven forty-seven," said Tracy, straining to make out the house numbers by the glow of Brad's headlights. "We're looking for twenty-seven fifty-three, which ought to be about—"

"It's there," Brad interrupted. "It's that house in the middle of the block. That Jaguar parked in front of it is Gavin's car."

"How can you tell?" Tracy asked doubtfully. "The house number is all faded out, and it's too dark to be able to see what color the car is."

"That's Gavin's car," Brad repeated firmly. "I'd recognize it anywhere."

He could remember the very first time he had seen

that car. He had come home from school to find it parked in the driveway, its metallic paint glinting silver in the afternoon sunlight. Gavin had bought it as a "birthday surprise for Laura," but Brad's mother had been too upset by the cost of the vehicle to be willing to even think about trying to drive it. Brad had been quickly proclaimed too young and inexperienced a driver to be allowed behind the wheel, so by default the car had become Gavin's own special baby.

Now Brad brought the Impala to a stop on the side of the street opposite the hated symbol of his stepfather's self-indulgence and switched off the engine and the headlights. Like the other houses in the subdivision, the one numbered 2753 was small and boxy and set close to the street. There were lights on inside, but the drapes that were drawn across the front window obscured any view of the interior.

"Tell me again what happened over there," Brad said.

"You've already had me go over it twice," said Tracy.

"Tell me one more time. I want every detail. Maybe there was something you missed."

"There aren't any other details. Jim Tyler didn't mention his roommate's name. The only way I learned the name of the brother-in-law was from overhearing Jim's side of a phone conversation. While he was busy on the telephone, I searched the apartment. There was no sign that a child had ever spent time there."

"But Mindy's picture was in one of the bedrooms?"

"Yes," said Tracy. "I'm certain, though, that she doesn't live there."

"Then Gavin has got to be keeping her somewhere else," Brad said. "That makes sense. It would be almost impossible to conceal a two-year-old in a singles apartment building. Kids Mindy's age don't like to stay cooped up inside."

"So where do you think Mindy is?"

"I'm not sure," said Brad. "All I know is, whatever it takes, I'm going to find her." He shoved the car door open. "I'll be back in a couple of minutes."

"Where are you going?"

"Just to check things out. Maybe I can find a side window that isn't curtained over."

"I'm coming with you," Tracy told him.

"It would be better if you didn't. One person is less likely to attract attention."

"I said I'm coming." She got out of the car and came around to stand next to him in the street. "I'm in this too. Don't forget, I'm the one who did the major part of the detective work."

"Okay," Brad said grudgingly. "Come on, then, but be careful not to make any noise. If the Carvers have a dog, we don't want to start it barking."

They crossed the street in silence. On the far side, Brad paused beside the parked Jaguar and impulsively placed his hand on the sleek silver hood. The metal surface was cool to his touch, but he was surprised to find that it was also dull and gritty. Back when Gavin had been a part of their Albuquerque household, he had been compulsive about keeping his car in mint condition.

Brad tried the door and found that it was not locked. He opened it, and the ceiling light flashed on, flooding the interior with an uneven yellow glow.

"See those boxes back there?" he said to Tracy, gesturing toward the rear seat stereo speakers. "There's a story behind those, and it isn't a pretty one. The morning Gavin was installing them, Mom left Mindy with him for a few minutes while she went out for groceries. He got so caught up in what he was doing that he forgot her. She came toddling up to the door and walked into his soldering iron. The poor kid's still got a scar across her belly."

"You'd better close the door," Tracy said nervously. "Somebody in the house might look out and see the light."

"They won't do that. Not with the curtains drawn."

The inside of the car seemed both familiar and strange to him. The walnut dashboard, in which Gavin had taken such pride, was coated with road dust, and the cream-colored upholstery was stained in several places, as though someone had tipped over a can of soda pop and not bothered to clean up the spill. The ashtray was full to overflowing with butts and ashes, and the carpet on the floor on the driver's side was littered with gum wrappers.

The state of the car's interior made Brad a bit less sure of the identity of its owner. Was it possible that it might not be Gavin's after all? When he told Tracy that he would recognize Gavin's car anywhere, he had spoken more with emotion than reasoned certainty. In the dark, cars of the same make and color were hard to tell apart, and a silver Jaguar, while unusual, was hardly unique.

Pulling the door open the rest of the way, Brad got into the car and slid across the seat to the passenger side. Since he had not been permitted to drive the sports car, he was unfamiliar with the possessions that were usually kept in it, but it was possible, he thought, that there might be something in the glove compartment that he would recognize as having belonged to his stepfather.

His first reaction upon opening the compartment was disappointment. Its only contents seemed to be road maps, a pack of cigarettes, some loose sticks of gum, and a misshapen candy bar that had melted and reformed itself inside its wrapper. Upon further investigation, however, he found what he was looking for. Buried beneath the pile of maps there was a brown manila envelope that contained the owner's manual and car registration.

With his heart beating faster, Brad removed the papers and held them under the light. The name on the registration was the one he had hoped to find there.

It's you! he exulted silently. I've tracked you down! You're in that house, and I bet you have Mindy with you!

He carefully returned the documents to the glove compartment and snapped it shut. Then he slid back across the seat and got out of the car.

"Well?" Tracy asked him. "Did you find anything?"

"It's Gavin's car, all right," Brad told her. "There's something odd, though, about the way he's stopped taking care of it. It's as though it doesn't matter to him the way it used to."

He eased the car door closed and without further conversation turned to lead the way across the lawn to the house. Skirting its darkened front, he continued on around to the far side of the building, where a shoulder-high hedge separated the Carver property from the lot next door. The grounds on this side of the house were mottled with pools of light cast by uncurtained windows; deep reservoirs of darkness lay between them. He tried to avoid the bright areas as best he could, and as a result found himself struggling to maneuver an obstacle course of metal trash cans and piles of firewood.

The first of the windows on this side of the house faced into the living room. It was a small, pleasant room, inexpensively furnished. Brad's mother would have referred to the decor as Leftover Newlywed. A set of brick and board bookshelves ran the full length of the room's back wall, and in the foreground a mismatched couch and chairs were arranged in a semicircle to form a conversation group around a tile-covered coffee table. The window was not wide enough to permit a full view of the room, but from what Brad was able to see it appeared unoccupied, although he thought he could detect the muffled sound of conversation filtering in from some adjoining area.

Silently, Tracy moved to stand beside him, stretching up on her toes to see over the window ledge.

"They must be back in the kitchen," she said. "Do you suppose they do have Mindy here?"

"I don't just suppose it, I *know* it," said Brad. "I see Bimbo."

"You see *what?*" Tracy asked in bewilderment.

"Bimbo, Mindy's bear. Can you see that brown thing on the floor over by the recliner? That's the teddy bear I gave Mindy on her very first birthday."

"You mean, Gavin kidnapped the bear as well as your sister!" Tracy said dubiously. "Why would he take the trouble to do that?"

"Bimbo's her favorite toy. She won't go anywhere without him. She must have had him with her when Gavin took her."

There was a short silence, during which they both continued to stare in through the glass at the unpopulated room, as though expecting a child to suddenly pop out of the woodwork.

Then, Tracy commented, "There's a horse in the hallway."

"A *horse?*" It was Brad's turn now to try to work his way into a better position at the window.

"Move over this way, and you can see it better," said Tracy. "It's one of those big plastic toys on springs that kids bounce on. Back in New York, I used to baby-sit for a lady in the apartment across the hall from ours. Her little boy had a horse like that."

"People don't cart a toy that size around with them," said Brad. "If it's here at the Carvers', that must mean this is where Mindy's staying. Her aunt must be taking care of her on a full-time basis."

Drawing back from the window, he turned and began to work his way farther along the side of the house, stumbling once and almost falling as his feet became tangled in a stray loop of garden hose. When he reached the second lighted window he came to a halt. Through it he could see a kitchen in which four people were gathered around a table, eating dinner. Standing well back in the shelter of darkness provided by the hedgerow, Brad drew in a sudden sharp breath.

"That's her!" he whispered. "That's Mindy!"

She was seated in a youth chair at the end of the table. Brad was taken aback at how much she had matured since he had seen her last. Her hair was pulled back and tied with a ribbon in an unfamiliar, young-ladyish style, and her face seemed to have lost much of its babyish roundness. Still, there was not a doubt in his mind that this was Mindy, four months older and lovelier even than he remembered her. The blue pajamas she was wearing accentuated the sky blue shade of her eyes, and her left cheek flashed its dimple as she smiled at her aunt.

"That's Mindy," Brad repeated softly, hardly able to believe it. It was all he could do to keep from rapping on the glass to capture the child's attention.

"Is the man with his back to us Gavin?" Tracy asked him.

"Yes," Brad told her without hesitation. He could not see the man's face, but the thick blond hair, the set of the shoulders, and the green and gold sports shirt his mother had given her new husband the first Christmas after they were married were all too familiar.

There was only one woman at the table, and she sat opposite the window. She seemed to be carrying on most of the conversation. She was slender and blond, and Brad had an excellent view of her face as she chatted along in an animated manner, directing her remarks to first one dinner companion and then another.

Gavin seemed to be the only one responding. The heavyset man who sat to the woman's left was concentrating on his food—fried chicken, Brad saw, and potatoes, and the type of mushed up green vegetable that Mindy had always hated, although tonight she seemed to be eating it with gusto.

"So what happens now?" asked Tracy. "Are you going to go in and get her?"

"You mean just go to the door and ring the bell? A lot of good that would do! There's no way they would ever let me walk in and take her. When it comes to muscle power, it would be two big guys against one small one. Gavin's brother-in-law is built like the Incredible Hulk."

"Why don't we go find a phone and call the police?"

"You've got to be kidding. And have them laugh in my face? After the way Lieutenant Souter sat back and did nothing for all those months, there's no way I'd trust the police to do anything to help me. Like I told you, they don't regard this as a kidnapping. If the person who runs off with the kid is one of the parents, they call it 'child-snatching,' and they don't take it seriously."

"What are you going to do then?" Tracy asked him.

"I don't know." He could not tear his eyes away from the sight of his sister, gnawing away on a drumstick and looking . . . contented. For some reason, he had not expected to find her happy. He had thought she would be suffering as he and their mother had been suffering, weeping herself to sleep at night, longing for her own bed in her own home—not complacently adjusting to life in an alien family.

What should he do next? He had been so riveted upon the challenge of locating Mindy that he had not planned for the second step of the recovery mission. How could he go about claiming her now that he had found her? Whatever he did would have to be sudden and drastic. To confront Gavin face to face would ruin everything. The moment he became alerted to the fact that he had been traced to Winfield, he would be up and gone, and Mindy would be lost forever.

Brad felt a sudden, gut-wrenching longing for Jamie, who could always be counted on for practical solutions.

"I have an idea," he said, keeping his voice carefully casual, as though taking Tracy's positive reaction for granted. "You could get Gavin's sister to hire you as Mindy's sitter. Then, while the Carvers were out, I could resnatch her."

"That's a great plan for *you*," said Tracy. "To me, it doesn't sound all that terrific. The Carvers come home, their niece is gone, and I'm the one held responsible. So *I* get charged with a felony, and you're home free."

"You wouldn't be charged with anything," Brad assured her. "You'd tell them I forced my way in and you couldn't stop me. They'd find you tied up or locked in a closet or something. Besides, the last thing these people would do would be to call the police. That would mean exposing Gavin, and they wouldn't do that."

"No," Tracy said firmly. "I just couldn't do that, Brad. What would happen if they didn't believe me? What if Doug Carver got violent? Helping you find your sister was a harmless adventure, but what you're suggesting now could be really dangerous."

From the sudden burst of activity within the kitchen, it appeared that dinner had now been officially declared over. Gavin's sister had risen from the table and was busily gathering up plates and carrying them over to the dishwasher. Her husband leaned back in his chair and patted his stomach.

Mindy said something to her father and started to

giggle. The dimple popped in and out of her cheek like a twinkling star. Gavin reached over and ruffled her hair, and the ribbon came loose, releasing a shining torrent of corn silk, which came tumbling down to frame the child's face.

Getting up from his chair, Gavin went around to Mindy's side of the table and bent to unfasten the safety strap on the youth seat. For the first time since their arrival, he was facing the window, and Brad had a full view of the man who had caused him so much anguish. His mouth filled with the sour taste of hatred, and he closed his eyes.

"I can't even stand to look at the bastard," he muttered.

There was a moment's silence. Then Tracy said, "Brad—he's *crying*!"

"Crying!" Brad exclaimed. "What would Gavin have to cry about?"

He opened his eyes and forced himself to stare at the man on the other side of the pane.

"He's not crying, Tracy, he's *laughing*. Mindy probably said something funny. You must have been looking at him through a warp in the glass."

"Maybe," Tracy conceded. She shifted her position at the window. "You're right—it wouldn't make sense for him to be crying. But when Mindy hugged him, it did look like he had tears in his eyes."

Chapter 8

The first thing Tracy was aware of when she entered the house on South Cotton Road that evening was the fact that the television set was not on. The sound of canned voices and laughter was so much a part of every night at the Stevensons' that without it the house seemed silent and oddly empty.

For a moment the possibility occurred to her that her aunt and uncle might have gone out to a movie or to visit friends. They did not do that often, but there were occasions when the urge to "live it up" would suddenly strike them and they would take off for a madcap two-hour "night on the town."

That hope was quickly squelched, however, when the couple emerged together from the living room, walking in tandem as usual and, with their identical serious expressions, looking more like Tweedledum and Tweedledee than ever. The main difference Tracy could see between the two of them was that her aunt's round face was pale and worried, while her uncle's was glowering and flushed with indignation.

"So, you've finally decided to come home!" Uncle Cory exploded. "Where in God's name have you been all this time?"

"I was out with a friend," Tracy told him. "We got busy talking, and I didn't realize how late it was getting to be."

"The fact that it's black as pitch outside might have given you a clue," her uncle said. "I can only suppose that this 'friend' was the same young man who kept you out so late last night. How could you lose track of time two nights in a row? How much do the two of you have to talk about, anyway?"

"I don't understand you people," Tracy countered defensively. "Aunt Rene made a big deal last night about how you want me to get involved in things like joining clubs and baby-sitting and going out on dates. Then to-night all I do is spend a couple of hours riding around in Brad's car, and the way you're reacting, you'd think the world's come to an end. Do you want me to have friends or don't you?"

"Of course we do, dear," Aunt Rene began in her usual placating voice. "What your uncle means is—"

"You don't have to explain the obvious, Rene," said Uncle Cory. "Tracy knows perfectly well that her social life is not the issue here. The point is, she never came home from school this afternoon, she never showed up for dinner, and she didn't even bother to call and check in. What we're talking about is nothing more than common courtesy. She could at least have phoned to let us know where she was."

"I'm sorry," said Tracy. "May I go to my room now, please? I have homework to do."

"You said you were sorry last night," her uncle continued, obviously having no intention of permitting the subject to be put to rest. "It's not as though we didn't go through this identical scene less than twenty-four hours ago. You knew perfectly well we'd be worried about you, yet you couldn't be bothered to make a simple telephone call to relieve our minds."

Tracy felt her own anger rising.

"Why should *you* worry?" she shot back at him. "You're not my parents, you're my landlords! My father's paying you to let me live in your home. There's nothing that says I have to eat every meal here."

She turned her back on them and started for the stairs.

"Come back here, young lady!" Uncle Cory bellowed after her. Then, when Tracy did not slow her pace, he continued angrily, "If hanging around with your new boyfriend generates this kind of rude behavior, then you'd better not plan on seeing him this weekend!"

Tracy continued on across the entrance hall without responding, ascended the stairs, and walked briskly down the length of the upstairs hall to her bedroom. She entered, flicked on the light, and very purposefully closed and locked the door.

Once inside the room, she was tempted to rush back out again. A flood of pink seemed to come rolling toward her from all directions, and for one dreadful moment she experienced the terrifying sensation that she was about to be suffocated by a cloud of rose petals.

Closing her eyes, she leaned back against the door and forced herself to fill her lungs with long drags of air. Slowly her anger at her aunt and uncle began to subside, and she felt drained and emotionally exhausted and a little guilty. On one level, she regretted the unpleasant scene downstairs, while on another, she was relieved at having let off steam. To be fair, she knew her relatives were dutiful people who had made a commitment and were doing their best to honor it. At the same time, the hypocrisy of keeping up the two-sided pretense that her current living situation was anything other than a business arrangement was becoming more and more difficult for her to deal with.

I just wish it were over! she thought. I wish I were graduating! How am I ever going to stand another whole year here!

She remained as she was until her heartrate had slowed and she was breathing normally again. Then she opened her eyes and took a survey of the room. As she had expected, her aunt had been in to "tidy up and make things nice." The window that Tracy had closed the night before now stood open, and the curtains were stirring gently in the evening breeze. The clothing she had worn the previous day had disappeared from the chair on which she had tossed it, presumably having been transferred to a bureau or closet. When she turned to the bed, she saw without surprise that it had been neatly made, its two pillows lined up symmetrically beneath an unwrinkled spread.

An envelope with a foreign stamp sat propped against one of the pillows.

Tracy went over to the bed and stood gazing down at it. For a moment she was tempted to rip it up, unread, and drop the pieces into the wastebasket. Then, as though she had no control over her own actions, she found herself sitting down on the bed, picking up the envelope, and opening it.

Inside there was a single sheet of hotel stationery, with the Trevi Fountain embossed in gold at its top left corner. Tracy drew the sheet of paper out of the envelope and unfolded it. "Dearest Daughter," the salutation read.

Richard Lloyd's *D*'s were artistically shaped, curling and looping with graceful abandon and culminating finally in a great dramatic flourish. In the days when professional rivalry was just beginning to infiltrate their marriage, Tracy's mother had liked to joke that, if her husband didn't make it in show business, he could always make a living putting monograms on bathrobes.

As Tracy remembered, her father had not thought that funny.

"I hope all's well in the good old Southwest," the letter continued:

I haven't had a word from you since arriving in Italy. I don't hold you to blame, of course, since mail service here is the pits, but I do hope I'll be getting a letter soon.

The filming's going well, and if nothing happens to slow things down, we will be putting the wraps on this picture in another six weeks. That should put you at the end of your school year. If one of those romantic Texas cowboys hasn't got you hog-tied, how about flying over to join me for some sight-seeing? We could start here in Rome and then move on to Florence. I'll have a month before I'll need to be back for the . . .

"One month out of the whole year!" Tracy murmured sarcastically. "That's so good of you, Dad—to sacrifice four whole weeks for your daughter!"

She crumpled the sheet of paper into a ball and pitched it in the direction of the wastebasket. Her hand was shaking with anger, and her shot went wild. The wad hit the rim, teetered there for a moment, and then tumbled in the wrong direction, landing on the carpet.

Tracy got up from the bed and crossed the room to the basket. She bent down and picked up the letter, holding it with two fingers as though she were disposing of a dead rodent, and dropped it into the trash receptacle.

"So much for that," she whispered, rubbing her hand on her jeans.

She went over to the window to pull down the blind.

It was still too early in the evening for the lights to be on in the second-floor windows of the house across the street. The lower windows were bright, however, and she could see a blur of color and movement as the occupants of the living room passed back and forth behind the glass.

Her mind flew back to the house on Sweetwater Drive. It had been a strange sensation to stand outside in the darkness and watch the dinner scene being played on a kitchen stage. Having grown up around the world of the theater, Tracy had spent many hours of her life watching professional actors practice their role playing. The experience tonight had been strange because there had been no dialogue, and as a result her attention had been concentrated on physical detail: on the dimple that appeared in the little girl's cheek when she smiled; on the affection on the face of the aunt as she cut the child's meat; on the look in Gavin's eyes when he bent to lift Mindy from the youth seat, the glint that the twisted window had portrayed as tears.

As Brad had said, Mindy's father had no reason for weeping. He was the cause of injury, not the recipient. Now that she had seen Mindy, Tracy could even better appreciate the incredible sense of loss her mother must be experiencing. It was ironic that Brad had managed to locate his sister only to find himself stymied by the problem of how to lay claim to her.

In the house across the street a light went on upstairs, and a couple of moments later the lights on the first floor went out.

Tracy closed her window and was just pulling down the blind when the quiet of the room was broken by a rap on the door.

Oh, no, Tracy thought. Not another good-night visit from Aunt Rene!

The thought occurred to her that perhaps, if she remained silent, her aunt would assume she was asleep and go back downstairs.

This did not work, however. When there was no response to the knock, the doorknob rattled pathetically, as the person on the far side of the door made an unsuccessful attempt to turn it.

"Tracy?" As she had expected, it was indeed her aunt. "Open this door! I told you last night I don't like for you to keep it locked. It isn't safe!"

With a sigh of resignation, Tracy did as instructed. She pulled the door partway open and stood with her body blocking the doorway, gazing defiantly out at the woman in the hall.

"I locked it because I wanted to be alone," she said. "I have a lot of studying I need to do."

"But you haven't had your dinner yet," Aunt Rene protested. "I have a plate already made up for you in the kitchen. It'll take just a minute in the microwave to heat it up."

"Thanks, anyway," said Tracy, "but I'm not hungry."

"Just some milk and cookies, then?"

"I said I'm not hungry."

There was a moment of silence. Then her aunt asked, "Did you find your letter?"

"Yes," Tracy told her.

"Was it from your father?"

"Of course it was from Dad," Tracy said impatiently. "You must have seen the return address on the envelope. Who else do we know who's currently living in Rome?"

"Did he say anything about making plans for the summer?"

"Nothing that mattered."

"Then he probably doesn't know yet what his work schedule is going to be."

"It doesn't matter what his schedule is," said Tracy. "I

don't want to visit him, and I don't want him coming here. I'll find something to do with myself so I won't be a drag on you and Uncle Cory. Maybe I could go to some sort of summer camp."

"I wish you wouldn't be so bitter about your father," said Aunt Rene. "I know you were disappointed when he didn't take you to live with him, but he had his reasons, and I'm sure he thought they were good ones." She paused. "It was distressing to me to hear you say the things you did tonight," Aunt Rene continued in an injured voice. "Your father insists on contributing to your support. The checks he sends are no more than the payments he used to send your mother. We didn't ask him to pay us, and we'd have taken you in regardless. We consider it a blessing to have you with us."

Tracy did not take the trouble to contest the statement. Instead, she said, "Uncle Cory said I couldn't go out with Brad this weekend. Does that mean I'm grounded from everything?"

"Why, no," Aunt Rene said. "It's only when you get with Brad that problems seem to develop. I suppose if you wanted to go out with some other boy—"

"I don't want to go out with any of the boys from Winfield," Tracy said. "What I was thinking about was baby-sitting. A friend of mine knows some people who need a sitter Friday night. If it's all right with you, I thought I'd apply for the job."

"I don't believe Uncle Cory would object to that," said her aunt. "Of course, we would want to know where it was you'd be sitting."

"The people's name is Carver," Tracy told her. "If they call you to check me out, will you tell them I'm responsible?"

"Of course," Aunt Rene said immediately. "You *are* responsible, dear. It's been just these past two evenings that you've acted thoughtlessly. Brad really doesn't seem to be a very good influence. I hope you're not going to let him cause problems in your life."

"I won't," Tracy assured her. "In fact, Brad won't be around much longer. He's going to be leaving soon to go live with his mother in New Mexico." She paused and then asked, "Is it all right if I call him? I promise I won't be on the phone more than a minute, but I do have to tell him that our plans for Friday have been changed."

Chapter 9

Brad was not at the Trade Winds to receive Tracy's call, and he did not find out she had phoned until the following morning. After he dropped her off at her house, he drove on to a Steak-In-the-Rough a few blocks from the high school and ordered a hamburger, fries, and a milk shake to go. Then, too filled with adrenaline to contemplate an early return to the motel, he drove to the shopping mall where he had seen the James Bond movie and picnicked in the darkened theater to the accompaniment of a double feature presentation of *Rocky III* and *Rocky IV*.

When he did, at last, get back to the Trade Winds, it was after midnight. He stripped off his clothes, took a shower, and got into bed. Almost at once he realized that sleep was not going to come easily. His mind was too busy churning with the events of the evening.

Incredible as it might seem, he had really found Mindy! Against all odds, despite all the negative predictions, he had found her! Lieutenant Souter had termed him crazy. His own mother had advised him to accept the fact that Mindy was gone forever. Even Jamie, the one person in the world he had always been able to count on, had told him, "It isn't going to work. You don't know what you're doing." But it *had* worked! He had *made* it work!

Tonight he had seen his sister, and when he returned to Albuquerque, she would be with him.

He could not wait that long to share the wonderful news. He was too excited, too triumphant! He considered phoning his mother, but decided against it; he did not want to ruin the glorious surprise. With Jamie, it was different. He just had to make contact with Jamie! It was only fitting that Jamie-of-little-faith should be the first to learn that what had so scornfully been termed "impossible" had been accomplished. Besides, Jamie might be able to provide some helpful suggestions. Within the context of their longtime friendship, it had always been Jamie who had been the down-to-earth partner, while Brad was the one who operated on inspiration and impulse.

Sitting up in bed, Brad switched on the light and reached for the telephone. His fingers knew the familiar number so well that they were already on the sixth digit before he remembered he was calling long distance and had to hang up and start over with the area code.

At the far end of the line the phone rang again and again. Finally, there was a click, and a sleepy voice said, "Hello?"

"Hello, Mrs. Hanson," Brad said. "I'm sorry if I woke you, but I need to speak to Jamie."

There was a moment of silence.

Then Jamie's mother said, "Brad, where are you? Jamie told me you were up in the Pecos fishing."

"I am," Brad said, the lie coming so easily and naturally that he did not even have to compose it. "I had to drive down to Terrero to pick up supplies, and I thought that while I was here I'd give Jamie a call."

"Are you all right?"

"What do you mean, am I all right?"

"It's the middle of the night," said Mrs. Hanson. "There aren't any stores open anywhere at this hour. Jamie's been asleep for hours. What's happened, Brad? Where are you really?"

"I told you," Brad said, exasperated with himself for having invited this interrogation. "I'm calling from a convenience store that's open all night. When you're out where there aren't any clocks, you lose track of time. I'm sorry I woke you. I didn't realize it was this late."

"Well, it is." She sounded irritated, but somewhat mollified. As the mother of three sons and a daughter, Mrs. Hanson was used to the foibles of teenagers. "This isn't an hour to call people for casual chats. Give me your number, and I'll have Jamie call you back in the morning."

"I don't have a phone," Brad said. "I'm staying up at my dad's cabin. Just tell Jamie . . ." He struggled to find the exact words that would get across a message that Jamie alone would understand. "Say I've got a wonderful catch, the catch I've been dreaming about. My mom's going to go out of her mind when she sees what I'm bringing home. Say . . ." He paused, then spoke the words that were in his heart. "Say I wish that Jamie were here to be in on this with me."

"Wait, Brad. Don't hang up," said Mrs. Hanson, her voice filled with maternal concern.

Brad realized that he had gone too far. "I'm going to get Jamie right now. You two do need to talk. I can tell there's something the matter—"

"There's nothing the matter," Brad insisted, interrupting her. "In fact, it's just the opposite. Everything's great—even better than great. Give Jamie my message, and I'll be back with my catch on the weekend."

He replaced the receiver on the hook, angry with himself for having made the call in the first place. He had been so zeroed in on the idea of talking with his friend that he had not realized how unreasonable the hour was.

Now the best he could hope for was that Mrs. Hanson would return to her bed without feeling compelled to fill his mother in on the phone call.

It was at least another hour before he was able to get to sleep, and, as had been the case the previous night, when he did at last drift off, his slumber was rampant with dreaming. With Mindy on the saddle in front of him, he was riding a child's bounce horse along the road leading back to Albuquerque. The hot dry air of the desert filled his nostrils, and the brilliant midday sun beat down upon his head. Fine strands of Mindy's pale hair blew back to tickle his face with silken fingers, and her shoulder blades felt fragile as bird wings against his chest.

A car horn blared behind them, and when he turned to look over his shoulder, he could see in the distance the glitter of silver reflecting the sunlight. "Faster!" he told the horse. "Faster!" He dug his heels into its hard plastic sides, and it put on a burst of speed that sent it flying along the highway, but the silver Jaguar was coming up behind even faster.

When the car drew opposite, Brad saw Jamie was behind the wheel.

"Go back!" Jamie yelled across at him. "I told you it wasn't going to work!"

"It *is* going to work!" Brad shouted. "We're almost home!"

He could see the city of Albuquerque looming up ahead of them—the Sunwest Bank Building, the downtown Convention Center, the public library. He could see the roof of his own home shining like a beacon, as though the roof were glass and it were lighted from within. The Jaguar passed them and then changed lanes to block the horse's path, but the giant springs on the animal's legs catapulted it skyward, and when it descended, the car was nowhere in sight.

"We're almost home!" Brad announced to Mindy. "See that building ahead? It's the Holiday Inn!" But, as he spoke, he suddenly realized the motel he was pointing out to her was not the Holiday Inn on the outskirts of Albuquerque, but the one he had passed when driving into Winfield. The building he had thought was the public library was Winfield High School, the bank building was Steak-In-the-Rough, and the house he had identified as his own was actually the Carvers' house on Sweetwater Drive. In the instant it took him to absorb this knowledge, Mindy vanished from his arms, and when he glanced frantically about for her, he saw Gavin standing by the side of the road, his hands extended in a gesture of helpless pleading and his face distorted by tears.

He was blasted into consciousness by the telephone on the bedside table. When he opened his eyes the room was gray with the light of morning, and the pipes in the bathroom were already alive and rattling. Fragments of his dream clung to his brain like wisps of cotton as, still numbed by sleep, he groped for the receiver.

The caller turned out to be the motel manager.

"You got a phone call last night at ten fifteen," he said. "The girl on the desk tried to ring you, but there wasn't any answer. Somebody named Tracy left you a message that she's got something important to tell you. She said for you to come by the school at lunchtime."

"By the school at lunchtime," Brad repeated, coming abruptly awake.

He was tempted to return the phone call, but decided against it. If the Stevensons had been upset by the fact that Tracy had not come home for dinner, there was no sense in making things worse by phoning the next morning.

Since B lunch was not until 12:30, he was left with five hours to kill. Too wide awake by this time to go back to sleep, Brad got out of bed, got dressed, and drove over to McDonald's. There he consumed two Egg McMuffins and washed them down with tinny-tasting orange juice. Then he got back in the car and, after driving aimlessly about for a while, found himself turning onto the highway that led to the east side of town.

This time he was able to locate the subdivision easily. He drove down Sweetwater Drive to the twenty-seven hundred block and pulled to a stop on the far side of the street from the Carvers' house, in the exact spot in which he had parked the night before.

In the light the house had a perky appearance that darkness had concealed. The trim along the edge of the roof was Wedgwood blue, and a row of hand painted Mexican tiles spelled out the street number. The yard was small but well kept and bordered by neatly trimmed hedges. The flagstone walkway leading from the sidewalk to the front steps was flanked by beds of hyacinths, daffodils, and tulips.

The garage door was closed, and there was no car parked in the driveway. Even though it was now daylight, the drapes were still drawn across the front window, making it difficult to tell whether anyone was in the house. The morning was bright and sunny, perfect for outdoor activity. If his sister was there, Brad thought, she might be in the back yard.

How ironic it would be if he could restage the kidnap scenario and steal Mindy back in the same way that she had been taken! Secure in the knowledge that the curtained window made seeing out as impossible as seeing in, Brad got out of the car and crossed the street. Following the same route that he had taken the night before, he walked along the side of the house opposite the hedgerow. The obstacles that had presented problems in the darkness was easily avoided in the light of morning. He moved quickly past the line of garbage cans and the woodpile and stepped over the tangled loops of garden hose.

At the corner of the house, he was disappointed to discover that his access to the area at the back was cut off by a chain link fence. On the far side of the metal mesh he could see a swing set and sandbox. There was no one in the yard, although a red tricycle parked by the kitchen door seemed to indicate that Mindy had recently been playing there.

"Are you looking for somebody?"

The voice burst out of nowhere so unexpectedly that his first impulse was to spin on his heel and run. Regaining control with effort, he turned slowly around.

A gray-haired woman was peering at him over the top of the hedge.

"If you haven't figured it out yet, nobody's home," she said.

"I rang the bell," Brad told her, hoping his nervousness was not too apparent. "When nobody answered, I thought I'd look out back and see if they were here."

To his relief, the woman seemed to accept that statement.

"You're Sally's brother, aren't you?" she said with a knowing nod. "I saw your car with the out-of-state license plates. Sally told me you'd moved out here from New Mexico. The way she talked though, I didn't expect you to be so young."

"Doug and Sally had me over last night for dinner," Brad told her. "I think I may have left my wallet. I was hoping my sister would be here and I could get it back from her."

"This is Sally's day to drive the nursery school car pool," the woman informed him. "She ought to be home any time now. If you want to come over to my place, I can give you a cup of coffee while you wait."

"Oh, no thanks," Brad told her hastily. "I've got to be getting on to work. I'll give Sally a call later today and see if I can pick up the wallet this evening."

Hurrying back to his car, he got in and drove off quickly.

The remainder of the morning he spent wandering about the shopping center, which by now seemed almost as familiar as the malls in Albuquerque. Then, at 12:15, he drove over to the high school, parked in the student lot, and waited there until the bell rang to signal the start of B lunch. He then entered the building and joined the flow of teenagers headed for the cafeteria. Once in the door, he bypassed the food line and went straight into the dining area, hoping he could spot Tracy before she attached herself to a group of fellow students.

Almost immediately he heard his name called.

Responding automatically, he turned to see Gina Scarpelli beckoning eagerly to him. She was wearing a purple sweater several sizes too small, and her hair tumbled over her shoulders like a platinum waterfall. A quick survey did not disclose Tracy as one of her table companions.

Brad gave her a casual wave, but, not satisfied with that, she continued to gesture to him to join her. Reluctantly, he gave in and went over to her table.

"So, where have you been?" she asked him by way of greeting. "Have you given up food for Lent? I haven't seen you in the lunchroom for two full days now."

"My schedule got changed," Brad told her. "I don't have B lunch anymore. I'm only here now because I'm trying to locate Tracy."

"You're looking for Tracy?" Gina's lips pursed in an

exaggerated pout of disappointment. "Didn't anybody ever tell you blondes have more fun?"

"I've heard that rumor," Brad said, struggling to dredge up the golden grin. It was hard to get his lips to curve into a smile. "It's Tracy, though, who took the Shakespeare course last semester. I was hoping she might still have her notes on *Macbeth*."

"She probably does," Gina said. "She's into theater and stuff like that. Did you know her father was Richard Lloyd, the movie star?"

"Yeah, I heard about that," Brad said. "You wouldn't happen to know where she is, would you? Since you're such good buddies, I thought I'd find the two of you together."

"Tracy and I aren't 'buddies,' " Gina corrected him. "We go around some at school because we share a locker, but the rest of the time we hardly see each other. When she moved here last fall, I tried to get a friendship going, but Tracy made it clear she wasn't interested in being close friends with anybody."

"But you usually *do* eat together," Brad persisted.

"She skipped lunch today. She said she had to make some phone calls." The tone of her voice changed and grew suddenly brighter. "Don't be a stranger, Brad. Everybody isn't a loner like Tracy. If you get lonesome, remember, we're the only Scarpellis in the phone book."

"I'll keep that in mind," Brad said. "Thanks for reminding me."

He left the cafeteria and immediately started down the hall toward the office. He had almost reached it when Tracy emerged from the doorway. She caught sight of him at the exact moment he saw her, and raised her hand in a gesture of greeting. "I was just trying to call you," she said as they drew abreast of each other. "Did you get the message I left for you at the motel?"

"I got it this morning," Brad said. "I almost phoned you back, but I thought that might not go over too well with your folks."

"You were right about that. My aunt's scared you're going to 'make problems' for me." She gave a short, mirthless laugh. "The truth is, she's probably right. I just got finished talking to Sally Carver. She's hired me to baby-sit tomorrow night."

"You did *what*?" Brad exclaimed, unable to believe his ears.

"I would have called her last night, but I thought it would be safer to wait until Jim Tyler had left for Padre Island. That way the Carvers can't check on how well he knows me."

"But, you told me you wouldn't do it," Brad said in bewilderment. "I didn't think there was anything that would change your mind."

"I didn't either," said Tracy, "but then last night I got a letter. It made me realize all over again how rotten fathers can be."

Chapter 10

Doug Carver arrived at the Stevenson house at 6:05 on Friday evening. Tracy, who had been hovering in the second-floor hallway, ready to make a dash down the stairs and out the front door the moment the doorbell rang, was disgruntled to find her aunt positioned in the entrance hall when she reached the foot of the staircase.

"I'm sure that's for me," Tracy said. "It's the people I'm baby-sitting for."

"You're probably right, dear," Aunt Rene responded agreeably. "That's why I came out from the kitchen. I'd like to meet them."

With a sigh of resignation, Tracy opened the door. She was greeted by the sight of the same heavyset man whom she had last seen seated at the dinner table in the Carvers' kitchen. Tonight, garbed for a more formal occasion, he was dressed in a suit and tie, and the collar of his dress shirt was clamped around his thick neck like a vise.

"Hi there," he said. "I'm here to pick up Tracy Lloyd."

"I'm Tracy," Tracy told him. She glanced over at her aunt, who stood waiting to be introduced, as placidly unbudging as a Jell-O pudding stuck in a mold. "This is my aunt, Irene Stevenson."

"Doug Carver, here. Pleased to meet you, Mrs. Stevenson." A huge paw was thrust out for Aunt Rene to shake.

"You look awfully familiar, somehow," she said. "You don't happen to live in the East Ridge subdivision, do you?"

"How did you know that?" Doug Carver regarded her with amazement.

"I'm the agent who sold you your house!" Aunt Rene said with a laugh, obviously tickled by his reaction. "As I recall, it was a charming little place with a maple tree in the back. I can even remember the street name—Sweetwater Drive."

"That was back when we were first married!" exclaimed Doug Carver. "With all the people you must meet in your line of work, how can you remember us?"

"Oh, I always remember the newlyweds," Aunt Rene said lightly. "How is your wife? Let me think now—her name was . . . Susie?"

"Sally," Doug corrected. "We're both of us doing just fine. In fact, tonight we're celebrating our fifth anniversary."

"And Tracy is going to be your sitter. Isn't that something! As I recall, when you bought your house, you weren't planning on a family."

"We got a surprise package," Doug said. "Life sometimes hands you those." He turned to Tracy. "Well, little lady, are you set to go?"

"All set," Tracy said, relieved to have the amenities done with.

"Then we'd better get a move on. We've got a lot planned for tonight, and Sal and I are running on a tight schedule. First we're having dinner at a restaurant with friends, and then we're going to a play at the Community Theater."

Once in the car with the engine running, Doug reached over to turn up the radio, which had burst into violent life with the twist of the ignition key. The drive out to the East Ridge subdivision was made to the accompaniment of country-western music played at top volume. By the time they pulled into the Carvers' driveway, Tracy's ears were numb and her head was throbbing.

Sally Carver was waiting just inside the doorway, looking surprisingly exotic for a Winfield housewife. She was wearing a forest green scoop-necked dress with gold accessories, and her blond hair was arranged high on her head in an intricate French braid.

She greeted Tracy cordially and then turned to her husband. "So you're finally back! What in the world took you so long? I told you we're meeting the Mahrers at a quarter to seven."

"I stopped to visit a minute with Tracy's aunt," Doug said. "Believe it or not, she's the real estate agent who sold us this house."

"That's coincidence number two then," Sally said. "The first was Tracy's calling us when she did, right when we were absolutely frantic about finding a sitter. All I can say is, blessings on Jimmy Tyler! He's an angel for having given you our number, Tracy."

"We'd better get the show on the road, hon," Doug broke in. "Is Cricket down for the night?"

"Probably," Sally said. "I tucked her in and handed her Monk-Monk and put on the *Songs From Dreamland* tape. That usually does the job in about thirty seconds."

"Cricket?" Tracy repeated the name in bewilderment. "Her name is *Cricket*?"

"It's a nickname," explained Doug. "You'd understand why if you ever saw her in the daytime. The kid's like a jumping bean. She never stops hopping around."

"You don't have to worry about her tonight though,"

Sally said reassuringly. "Once she hits that bed, she's down for the count. Around ten, you'll have to get her up and walk her to the bathroom. She sleeps so soundly she won't wake up on her own until the bed's wet.

"Cricket's room is down the hall, second door on the right. If you should need to get hold of us for any reason, the information about where we'll be is on a pad by the telephone. Help yourself to anything you want from the refrigerator." She looked at her watch. "Doug, we've really got to get going!"

"That's what I've been trying to tell you," Doug Carver responded in mock exasperation. "Tracy doesn't need a thirty page instruction sheet. Next thing, you'll be offering to supply her with a floor plan of our home."

They were still engaged in lighthearted bantering as they left the house. Tracy stood gazing out through the screen as they crossed the yard and got into their car. The engine roared to life and the car radio followed suit, filling the evening with foot-stamping bluegrass. The headlights flashed on like the eyes of a waking cat as Doug backed the car slowly out of the driveway and into the street.

Tracy continued to stand and watch until the Carvers had disappeared from sight around a bend in the road and Sweetwater Drive had settled back into undiluted darkness. Then, closing the door but leaving it unlocked, she went down the hall to the room in which the child was sleeping.

The bedroom door had been left standing open, and light from the overhead in the hallway spilled into the room, illuminating the small figure on the bed. Mindy was lying on her side with her thumb in her mouth. Her silken hair was spread out across the pillow like a halo. With her free hand, she was clutching a toy monkey, and a tape recorder on the floor by the bed was playing softly. A woman's voice was singing a song about the moon.

"Mindy?" Tracy asked softly. "Are you awake?"

The child made no response.

"The moon is wise, the moon is old, and all her songs come wrapped in gold," sang the lady on the tape.

Tracy switched on the lamp on the bedside table. Despite the fact that Mindy was a recent addition to their household, it was evident that the Carvers had redecorated the room for her. The wallpaper was splashed with pictures of brightly colored balloons, and the curtains were adorned with *Sesame Street* characters. A throw rug on the floor was in the shape of Big Bird.

Crossing to the bureau, Tracy pulled open the topmost drawer. It was filled with panties, socks, pajamas, and T-shirts. She began removing the clothing, stack by stack, placing it in neat piles on the top of the chest of drawers. When the first drawer had been emptied, she shoved it closed, pulled out the one below it, and began to remove the clothes from that.

"The sweetest songs I ever knew; she has no child to sing them to," crooned the lullaby lady. "Poor lonely moon, poor Mother Moon. . . ."

Gentle as it was, the voice on the tape was loud enough to cover the sound of the front door opening, and although she had been expecting him, Tracy was startled when Brad appeared suddenly in the doorway to the bedroom.

"I was parked down at the corner and saw the car drive off," he said. "They sure took their own sweet time about leaving the house. I was beginning to be afraid they might have changed their minds about going out." He paused. "What are you doing over there?"

"I'm getting Mindy's things together," Tracy told him.

"You don't have to do that. She's got plenty of clothes back in Albuquerque," said Brad. "Mom was going to give all her stuff to Goodwill, but I wouldn't let her. I made her put it in boxes and store it in the attic."

"That was close to half a year ago," Tracy reminded him. "It's not likely many of those things will fit her now."

"You may be right. She sure has grown a lot." He went over to the bed and stood staring down at the sleeping child. "She's beautiful, isn't she? Like a princess in some fairy tale. I can't wait to see Mom's face when I walk through the door with her."

"The Carvers have a nickname for her," said Tracy. "They call her Cricket, because she's always hopping around."

"That's stupid. What do they think she is, a bug?" He reached down and smoothed back a lock of hair from the little girl's forehead. "Mindy's such a pretty name, why would anybody change it?"

"There'll be plenty of time to admire her later," said Tracy. "What you'd better do now is find something we can put these clothes in. It doesn't have to be a suitcase; any sort of sack or bag will do. And while you're at it, see if you can locate her bear."

"Doesn't she have him in bed with her?"

"She's sleeping with a monkey."

"That's odd," said Brad. "It used to be she wouldn't go to bed without Bimbo. She'd throw a fit if we tried to get her to sleep with any other toy." He bent closer to examine the object his sister was clutching to her chest. "You're right, though, it *is* a monkey. That doesn't make sense. I wonder why she took that shabby thing to bed with her."

He left the room and returned a few moments later with his arms loaded with brown paper sacks, which he placed on a chair next to the bureau.

"I found these in a storage room off the kitchen," he said. "Now I'll check around for Bimbo."

"Maybe you didn't see a bear the other night," Tracy suggested. "That lump on the floor could have been almost any toy. Neither of us could see very well through the window."

"It was Bimbo," Brad said firmly. "I know that bear. After all, I'm the one who went out and bought him."

Alone once again, Tracy continued with the task of removing Mindy's clothing from the second drawer and loading it into the grocery sacks. Then she pulled open the third drawer and emptied that also. The lullaby tape came to an end and the recorder switched itself off.

With the cessation of the music, the only sound in the room was the even breathing of the child on the bed. This time, when the front door opened, Tracy heard it perfectly. There was another short silence, during which she tried desperately to convince herself that she had been mistaken about the source of the sound. Then Doug Carver's voice exploded into the quiet.

"Who are you, and what are you doing in my home?"

Shocked into a state of paralysis, Tracy stood frozen, her hands convulsively clutching the straps of a pair of tiny overalls that she had been preparing to drop into the second half-filled sack.

If there was a response to Doug's question, it was not discernible from the bedroom.

Doug's voice rose again in an outraged bellow.

"Tracy Lloyd! You get yourself out here this minute!"

The sound of her name released Tracy from immobility. Letting the overalls fall to the floor, she rushed out of the bedroom and hurried down the hall to the living room.

The scene that confronted her there was even worse than she had anticipated. Huge and glowering, Douglas Carver was planted solidly in the center of the room in the stance of a bull preparing for a charge. His head was lowered, and his nostrils were flared and quivering. In one crazy instant of near hysteria, Tracy could almost imagine that he was going to begin to snort and paw holes in the carpet.

Brad was standing across from him in the doorway to the kitchen, looking as startled and caught off guard as a matador who had misplaced his sword and sent his red cape to the cleaners.

As Tracy entered the room, Doug swung around to confront her.

"You call yourself a *baby-sitter?*" His voice was shaking with fury. "We haven't been gone twenty minutes, and already you've let a stranger into our house! You were hired to take care of Cricket, not to entertain visitors!"

"It isn't the way it looks. I mean, Brad is a friend of mine." Tracy groped frantically for words to explain the unexplainable. "I didn't know—I mean, I thought . . ." Unable to come up with a way to end the sentence without revealing the true reason for Brad's presence there, she let it trail off uncompleted.

"I *know* what you thought," Doug said grimly. "You thought we were gone for the evening and you and your boyfriend could have the run of the house. Well, it didn't work out that way, did it? As it turned out, I forgot our theater tickets, and I left Sally at the restaurant to order while I drove home to get them. The last thing I expected to find was a strange car in our driveway."

"I'm sorry," said Tracy—sorry you came back and saw Brad's car, she finished silently.

"Well, you'd *better* be sorry! This is the last time you baby-sit at *this* house!" Doug glared at her and then turned his attention back to Brad, who had not moved throughout the course of the diatribe. "As for you, kid, I want you out of here, and I mean *now!* You can count yourself lucky I'm not calling in the police."

There was a moment of silence.

Then, Brad said, "Maybe you should. If you want to call the cops, I wouldn't mind talking to them."

"Did I hear you right?" Doug demanded. "You *want* to be arrested?"

"I wouldn't be arrested," Brad said. "What law have I broken? *You're* the one who could be charged as an accomplice to a felony."

"Are you on drugs or something? You're talking like your brain's been fried." Doug regarded the boy with undisguised disgust. "I'm going to repeat this one time and one time only—*I want you out of my house!* If you don't walk out that door, I'm throwing you through it, and, believe me, little man, I'm the guy who can do that!"

In the terrible silence that followed, Tracy could hear the trip-hammer pounding of her heart, so loud in the room she was sure that the others heard it also. She could feel Doug's fury radiating out of him in waves like the energy-charged vibrations from an overheated motor.

She would not permit herself to look at Brad.

"Please," she said in a shaky voice, "do as he says. He's so much bigger than you. He could really hurt you."

For a moment she was afraid he was going to ignore her and continue to blurt out statements that would antagonize Doug Carver further. Then, like a windup toy activated by a switch, Brad stalked over to the door, jerked it open, and stepped out into the night.

His footsteps clicked twice on the doorstep and then were lost in the grass of the lawn. A few moments later, Tracy heard the slam of his car door.

Gentler sounds then suddenly rushed in to fill the void left by angry voices, filtering through the screen to invade the silent living room: the tinkle of wind chimes in a tree in the Carvers' front yard; guitar music wafting across from a neighbor's house; cicadas serenading springtime from their home in the hedge that separated the Carvers' house from the one next door.

Apparently satisfied that Brad had been permanently disposed of, Doug addressed himself to Tracy. "Your boyfriend's crazy. God knows what junk he's been shooting up or smoking. I can't believe you'd let someone like that come into this house with Cricket here." He paused and then, with a major effort, got a grip on himself and managed to continue in a calmer voice. "Now, I want you to get on the phone and call your aunt."

"Call my aunt?" Tracy repeated. "Why should I do that?"

"You're a minor, right? And Irene Stevenson's your guardian?"

"Yes," Tracy acknowledged.

"Then she's responsible. You've contracted to do a job you're not trustworthy enough to handle, so it's up to your aunt to take over in your place."

Tracy stared at him, unable to believe what she was hearing.

"You expect Aunt Rene to come over here and babysit?"

"Damn right I do," Doug said tersely. "Tonight's our anniversary. Sally and I have a celebration planned, and I'm not about to let you wreck it. I'll be too late to get back to the restaurant in time for dinner, but at least I can join my wife and friends at the theater. You get your aunt on the phone and explain what's happened. Tell her I'm not leaving this house until she gets here."

With no option but to obey, Tracy crossed to the telephone, which was situated on the table at the end of the sofa. She picked up the receiver and reluctantly dialed the number of the Stevensons' home. As the phone on the other end of the line began to ring, she could visualize her aunt and uncle, comfortably planted in front of the television, squabbling good-naturedly about whose turn it was to get up and answer.

The loser this time turned out to be her uncle. After the eighth ring it was his voice that said, "Hello?"

Before Tracy could respond, however, Brad spoke from the doorway. "Hang up, Tracy," he said. "You don't have to make that call."

Turning to face the door, Tracy could see the outline of his figure, a blurred shape on the far side of the screen. She drew in a sudden, sharp breath and lowered the receiver.

"Hello?" Uncle Cory's voice crackled, tiny and thin, at the end of the wire. "Hello? Who is this? Hello? Hello?"

Doug Carver said hoarsely, *"My God, the kid has a gun!"*

Tracy set the receiver back in its cradle.

Chapter 11

Brad pulled the screen door open and stepped into the room, keeping the hunting rifle leveled at the big man's chest.

"Yes, the kid's got a gun," he said. "Keep your hands at your sides and don't try anything stupid."

"I was right! You *are* crazy!" Doug Carver's normally florid face had turned the color of ivory. "Put that thing down, you idiot. It might accidentally go off."

"If it goes off, it won't be an accident," Brad said evenly. "I've done a lot of hunting with this gun, and I know how to use it." The pressure of the gun butt against his shoulder was reassuringly familiar. It brought back memories of deer trails in the Pecos Wilderness; of the pungent odor of dew-drenched pine needles in the early morning; of his father, turning to smile at him over his shoulder, his breath rising from his nostrils in little puffs of steam in the cold mountain air. "Do just as I tell you. Walk backwards into the kitchen."

Out of the corner of his eye he could see Tracy move away from the telephone table. Her face was pale, and she was staring at him incredulously.

"What are you doing?" she asked in a whisper. "Where did you get that thing?"

"Stay back out of the way," Brad warned her. "I don't want to run the risk of having you block my shot. If you get between us, you're probably going to get hurt." With the gun still trained on Doug, he began to advance slowly toward him. "Didn't you hear what I said? Get into the kitchen. That's the way"—as the man took one cautious step backward and then another."Keep moving back until you're through the doorway. Now, turn to your left."

"If this is a robbery, you're not going to get much," said Doug. "We're not rich people. There's no money stashed around here. All you're going to find in my wife's jewelry box is cheap imitation stuff. The only good pieces she owns are what she's wearing tonight."

"I don't want your wife's jewelry," Brad said. "I only want what's mine."

"If you're looking for drugs—"

"Stop talking and keep on walking."

He moved steadily forward, keeping pace as Doug backed into the adjoining room. Across from them, on the far side of the kitchen, the window he and Tracy had peered through two nights before reflected the activity in the lighted room. In its depths he could see Doug's broad back, encased in a gray pin-striped suit jacket, and beyond that, a slender, curly-haired boy holding a deer rifle. The boy's face looked foreign to him, steely-eyed and oddly expressionless—the face of a stranger he had never seen before. At the same time, he knew the person with the gun was himself and that the unnatural effect could be attributed to the warp in the windowpane.

"What now?" Doug asked grimly. His voice was stiff with anger, but beneath that there ran an unmistakable undercurrent of fear.

Brad glanced quickly about him, trying to decide on the next step. When he had confiscated the grocery sacks, he had not bothered to fully close the door to the pantry.

It now stood ajar, disclosing three walls of floor-to-ceiling shelving stocked with cleaning supplies, canned goods, and boxes of baking mixes.

"Get in there," he said. "Turn around and step through that door."

"You want me to go into the pantry?"

"That's what I said, isn't it?"

Doug seemed unable to decide whether or not to obey.

"Look," he said, "there's a little girl back in one of our bedrooms. I don't care what you do to me or how much stuff you take, but I want you to promise you won't do anything to her."

"I told you," Brad said, "I'm only going to take what's mine."

"She sleeps soundly," Doug continued. "She's not going to wake up. There's no reason you'd even want to go in there. There's nothing in that room you'd be interested in taking. It's just little-kid stuff, like picture books and toys."

"Get into the pantry," Brad told him, at the end of his patience. "If you push me any further, you're going to be sorry."

Glowering with fury and frustration, Doug did as directed and stepped through the doorway into the tiny, windowless storage room. His shoulders grazed the edges of the shelves on either side.

"You won't get away with this." His voice was muffled by the closeness of the room. "Why don't you quit while you're ahead, kid? We'll chalk this one up to the fact that you're high on something and aren't in any condition to be held responsible. I give you my word, I'm not going to call the police. You can walk out of here, and it'll be like nothing ever happened."

Not deigning to dignify the statement with a verbal

response, Brad thrust out his foot and kicked the door closed. The slam of it jolted the kitchen like a crack of thunder.

Instead of the usual punch button lock, this door had a bolt lock at shoulder height. Brad reached up and slid the bolt into place.

"Tracy?" he called. "Come out here! I need your help."

Tracy appeared in the doorway, visibly shaken. Her eyes were wide and frightened, and she glanced apprehensively about her as though she expected to be confronted by a scene of bloody horror.

"That noise!" she said. "When I heard it, I thought you'd shot him!"

"That was the sound of the pantry door," Brad told her. "The blast of a gun is a lot louder than that."

"This wasn't supposed to be part of it," said Tracy. "If you'd told me you had a gun, I'd never have agreed to this."

"The gun was my dad's," Brad said. "I had it in the trunk of the car. The way things worked out tonight, it's lucky I did."

"Put it down. It makes me nervous just seeing you hold it." Her voice had a sharp edge to it. "You wouldn't really have used it, would you? No matter what he did, you'd never have *shot* him?"

"I don't know," Brad told her honestly. He thought back upon the moment when Doug Carver had hesitated at the door to the pantry. If instead of obeying his command the man had attempted to rush him, would he have had the nerve to pull the trigger?

"I don't know," he said again. He set the stock of the gun on the floor and propped the tip of the muzzle against the kitchen wall. "That flimsy door won't hold if the Hulk tries to force it. We're going to have to pull the table over to brace it."

The dinette table had a butcher-block top, and there was a double-leaf insert attached beneath it, which made it a great deal heavier than it appeared on first glance. Even with Tracy's assistance, it took more effort than he had anticipated to haul it across the room and shove it tightly against the pantry door. Then they went back for the chairs and brought them over also.

By the time the job had been completed, the two black hands on the Garfield clock that hung over the refrigerator were indicating the time to be well past seven. Beyond the window, a thin slice of moon had ascended above the rooftop of the house next door and settled into the sky like a misplaced jewel in a witch's hair. The lighted kitchen reflected in the glass produced the illusion of an eerie second dimension, as though two unrelated photographs had been superimposed one upon another.

"We need to get a move on," Brad said. "Having Carver come back for those tickets screwed up our timing. His wife is going to be calling to see what's keeping him. When she doesn't get any answer, she's going to panic."

"I haven't finished packing yet," Tracy told him.

"Don't worry about that. Mom can buy her new stuff. The important thing now is to get Mindy out of here."

With Tracy at his heels, he went swiftly down the hall to Mindy's bedroom. After the loud scene in the living room, he half expected to find his sister awake and crying. To his relief, however, she was still sleeping soundly, curled in the same position in which he had left her, thumb in mouth, stuffed toy clutched to her heart.

When he bent to lift her from the bed, she emitted a soft kitten-mew of sleepy protest. Then, as Brad gently worked her free of the tangled bedclothes, she pulled her thumb out of her mouth with a popping sound and, with her eyes still closed, slid one arm around his neck. With her free hand, she continued to cling to the monkey.

"Mindy," Brad whispered, "do you know who's got you? It's Brad. I've come to take you home to Mommy."

She was as unexpectedly heavy as a sack of wet feathers, and she smelled of talcum powder and toothpaste and baby shampoo. The warm, limp weight of her body, the tickle of her hair against his cheek, the small sigh of her breath as she buried her face in the curve of his neck had been so long unexperienced that the new reality of them brought him close to tears.

It was strange to recall there had once been a time when he had not wanted her, when he had tried with all his mental strength to wish her out of existence. He could remember the shock he had experienced when his mother, pale-faced and teary-eyed, had broken the news to him that she was pregnant.

"This wasn't my idea," she had told him bitterly. "The last thing I ever wanted was to go through childbirth again. Gavin has this selfish need to prove his masculinity —and of course my feelings have never meant anything to anybody."

Throughout his mother's pregnancy, Brad had made a concentrated effort to avoid looking at her. It had horrified him to see her slim body grow increasingly thicker as the existence of the baby within her became more and more apparent. When Jamie had teased him about his upcoming role of "big brother," he had put the conversation to rest with such a blistering retort that his friend had never dared mention the subject again.

In the end, though, it had not been at all what he expected. His mother's labor had been short and the birthing experience comparatively easy. Mindy had been a Christmas baby, born right at the peak of the holidays, and she had come home from the hospital wrapped in a bright red blanket with a Santa Claus cap the size of a mitten on her round, bald head.

From the first moment he had laid eyes on her, garbed in her silly, festive outfit, he had blocked from his mind the thought that Gavin was her father. Instinctively, he had extended his finger to touch her, and immediately her tiny hand had closed around it. He had been amazed at the strength of the grip of her doll-size fingers, and the way she stared up at his face as if she already knew him. His heart had filled with a sudden rush of tenderness, and he had known, in that moment, he *wanted* to be a brother.

"What's the matter, Brad?" Tracy's voice snapped him back to the present. "You're the one who said we had to get out of here fast."

"We do," Brad said. "Do you think Mindy's going to be warm enough? Maybe we ought to take a blanket to wrap around her."

"I'll get one, and a pillow so she can sleep in the car. If you can handle one of these sacks, I'll take the other."

"And the gun," Brad said, raising his left elbow so Tracy could wedge one of the bags of clothing under it. "I left it leaning against the wall in the kitchen. Oh, and on your way back through the living room, take the phone off the hook. That should buy us some time when Carver's wife tries to call here."

Leaving Tracy to deal with the final aspects of their departure, he shoved the screen door open with his shoulder and carried Mindy out into the gentle darkness of the April evening. The night air was filled with the fragrance of hyacinths blooming in the flower beds along the walkway, and the cicadas in the hedge chattered sociably like friendly gossips.

When he had come out to the car earlier to retrieve

the gun, he had been too preoccupied to notice where Doug Carver had parked. He was happy now to discover that the Carvers' car was not blocking his own in the driveway, but was sitting instead at the curb in front of the house.

Except for that unoccupied car, the street was empty.

At the edge of the driveway, Brad let the paper sack slide out from under his arm so he could use his left hand to open the back door of the Chevy. As he was settling Mindy on the seat, he heard the door to the house slam closed, and a moment later Tracy joined him at the car. Her arms were piled with a blanket and a pillow and the second bag of clothing and she was gripping the rifle gingerly with both hands.

Brad took the sack from her arms and tossed it onto the floor of the car, and then he took the gun and laid it carefully on top. He spread the blanket over Mindy. "That does it," he said. "So, good-bye, Winfield!"

"Haven't you forgotten something?" Tracy asked quietly. "What's going to happen to *me* when you take off with Mindy? Doug knows now that the two of us were in this together. The plan about leaving me tied up here isn't going to work."

"I haven't forgotten about you at all," Brad said hastily, realizing with a rush of guilt that he had done just that. His mind had been totally occupied with his sister. "Of course you can't stay here," he improvised. "You'll be coming with us."

"All the way to New Mexico?"

"Is there any reason not to?"

Tracy considered a moment and then shook her head.

"No, I guess there isn't. There's nothing to hold me here. My aunt and uncle will probably be relieved to get rid of me."

"Then, get in," Brad said. "We've got a lot of ground to cover."

He opened the front door of the car and slid in behind the wheel.

Tracy got in beside him, and he started the engine.

Chapter 12

I don't understand it. Doug should have been back long before this." Sally Carver threw a worried glance at the steak and baked potato that sat cooling in front of the empty seat across from her. "His dinner's going to be ruined by the time he gets here. I can't imagine what's keeping him."

"Maybe he couldn't find the tickets," Kenneth Mahrer suggested, shoveling a forkful of french fries into his mouth.

"He said he knew where they were—or, at least, he thought he did. I wonder if I ought to try calling again."

"You've already called home twice, and the line's been busy both times. That must mean Doug's left the house and is on his way back over here." Kerry Mahrer reached across and gave her friend's hand a reassuring pat. "No sitter would have the nerve to stay on the phone like that if her employer was right there watching her do it. Who is sitting tonight, the Arquette girl again?"

"No, Katie takes driver's ed on Fridays," said Sally. "We're using somebody new, a friend of Gavin's roommate. We'd planned at first for Gavin to stay with Cricket. Then, the other evening, some girl called while he was at our place and invited him to go to a concert tonight. Of course, Doug and I encouraged him to accept. As depressed as he's been, he needs to get out and do things."

"It's hard to imagine being depressed at the Continental Arms," Kenneth remarked. "From what I've heard, that's heaven on a platter for singles."

"That's why we suggested Gavin move in there," said Sally. "A young bachelor who works with Doug was looking for a roommate, and we hoped life in a singles atmosphere might lift Gavin's spirits." She laughed ruefully. "A great idea, but it didn't work. Gavin's so wrung out he couldn't care less about dating. He spends all his free time at our house, mooning over Cricket."

"He seems to be awfully attached to her," Kerry commented.

"Far too attached to be healthy, in Doug's and my opinion. He needs to put the past behind him and start his life over. That's why we were so pleased when that girl invited him out. We felt it was important for him to go."

"If he's that much of a homebody, why didn't he stay married?"

"That marriage was a lost cause right from the start," Sally said. "I think the only reason Laura married my brother was because she couldn't exist without a man to take care of her. You've never seen such a helpless female in your life. She thinks the term 'woman's movement' means a trip to the beauty parlor. Nothing Gavin did for her was ever good enough. When he took her on a cruise of the Bahamas for their honeymoon, she wouldn't go out on deck for fear she'd get sunburned. When he bought her a sports car for her birthday, she refused to drive it because it 'made her nervous.' She complained about Gavin so constantly to that son of hers that the kid considered his stepfather some sort of ogre."

"What a shame!" exclaimed Kerry. "He'd probably have made that boy a wonderful father."

"Of course he would. That's obvious from the way he dotes on Cricket. It was Gavin who suggested he and Laura have a baby of their own. He thought if they had a child together, it might cement the family. That was another fine plan that didn't work out. According to Gavin, the boy got weird once the baby came. He acted as though she were his mother's and his private property. All Gavin was allowed to be in that family was a wage earner."

Sally nibbled at an unbuttered roll and glanced at her watch. "On the subject of cars, do you suppose Doug might have had car trouble?"

"If that had happened, he'd have had us paged," said Kenneth. "Poor guy, he's sure missed out on one fine meal. We'd better get the waitress to pack it up in a doggie bag."

"I bet he'll arrive within the next few minutes," Kerry said optimistically. "Let's order coffee and talk about something pleasant. Tell me, Sal, how is Cricket enjoying nursery school?"

"I called again, and the phone's still busy," Irene Stevenson told her husband, sinking down into the armchair across from his.

"She's probably telling Brad how unreasonable we are. That's the sort of teenage discussion that could last for hours."

"You're sure it was Tracy who called?"

"No, I'm not sure, Rene. I only told you I thought it *might* have been Tracy." Cory Stevenson pressed his right thumb against the channel turner, and the picture on the TV screen changed abruptly from a red-haired boy brushing his teeth to a cat eating Meow Mix. "There was a man's or boy's voice in the background. I thought I heard him say Tracy, but maybe he didn't."

"It might have been somebody talking on television," said Rene. "There's no reason for Tracy to call here and hang up without having said anything. That would be a senseless thing for her to do."

"You're right about that. What do you want to watch?"

"Anything. It doesn't matter." She paused and then continued, "Tracy's not stupid, Cory. She doesn't do senseless things."

"Missing dinner without checking in with us, I'd call that pretty senseless. She had to know it was going to get her in trouble."

"I wish you hadn't thrown such a scene," said Rene.

"She's living here now. She has to conform to our rules."

"Maybe we're being too strict. After all, we've never been parents before."

"And we're not parents now," Cory said. "She made that point in no uncertain terms—'My father's paying you to let me live in your house.' She considers herself our tenant, not part of our family."

"She's so bitter," Irene said with a sigh. "It's frightening to see a young girl so bitter. She made up her mind before she ever got here that she was going to hate Winfield and everybody in it."

"She misses her mother."

"Of course she does, poor dear. That's natural enough. What concerns me, though, is the way she's built her mother up in her mind to the point where she remembers her as too perfect to have been human. Danielle was talented and beautiful, it's true, but she did have faults. She never could stand to be overshadowed by anybody. Even back when we were children, if I ever owned anything she didn't, Dani would find some way of wrecking my pleasure in it.

"I remember one time—now this is going to sound silly—I spent three weeks' allowance on a box of underpants. Those were the days when little girls wore white cotton underwear, but these panties were all the colors of the rainbow. Sad to say, they also had the days of the week embroidered on them, which was something I hadn't realized when I bought them. Danielle made terrible fun of me in front of our school friends. She'd say, 'Pull up your dress, Rene, and let's see what day it is.' It wasn't long before I started hating those panties. I ended up dropping them into the incinerator."

"You think Richard left her because she made fun of his underwear?"

"Cory, stop teasing. I'm serious; I do think that trait of hers had something to do with why their marriage ended. She couldn't stand it that Richard's career took off faster than hers did. The way she treated that man during the last year they were together, I wasn't surprised at all when he finally divorced her."

"After Danielle died, I'd have thought Richard would have jumped at the chance to take Tracy to live with him," Cory said. "Especially when he had tried so hard to get custody."

"He seems to have matured a lot since the time of their divorce," Rene said. "Dani's murder brought home the fact that the world can be a dangerous place. No responsible father would leave a teenage girl alone in a city like Los Angeles while he spent months at a time away on location."

"You think that's why he let us have her?" asked Cory.

"Yes, I do," Rene said. "Danielle's death was a terrible shock to him. I don't think he'd ever really stopped loving her. Calling that night to ask us if we'd take Tracy was probably the hardest thing Richard ever had to do. I'm sure he'd love to have his daughter with him, but he thinks we can give her a safer, stabler home life."

"Well, we're trying our best."

"Yes, we are, but a lot of good it's doing!" She sighed and then said abruptly, "I know this is dumb, but I'm really worried about that funny phone call."

"It probably wasn't even Tracy." Cory flicked the turner again. The cat disappeared from the screen, and a man with a child on his lap came on in its place. The man was white, and the child was black, and they were smiling at each other.

Cory said, "That's Arnold, isn't it?"

"No, I think it's Webster. There are so many shows about people adopting children, and they all seem so happy and well adjusted. What's wrong with us that Tracy isn't able to love us?"

Cory Stevenson flinched at the note of pain in her voice. "It's not us, Rene, it's Tracy. She can't love anybody. There's too much hurt and anger bottled up inside of her. Maybe someday something will happen to break down that wall she's put up around herself, but until then, she's not going to let anybody get through to her. We've just got to keep on doing the best we can and hope she knows we're here for her if she needs us."

"I'm going to call the Carvers again," Rene said. "If the line's still busy, I think we ought to drive over there."

"You know how mad that will make her."

"I want to go anyway. I have this feeling something isn't as it should be."

"What a mother hen you are, Rene!" her husband said fondly.

He pressed another button on the box in his hand, and the television set went dark.

"Ed, do you know where Jamie is?" asked Barbara Hanson.

"Out in the garage, working on the car, I think." Her husband glanced up from the sports section of the evening paper. "Have the boys run out again without cleaning up the kitchen?"

"No, it's not that. They got the dishwasher loaded. There's just something I feel I ought to discuss with Jamie."

Barbara went back into the kitchen and out through the utility room door to the garage. The ceiling light was on, and as Ed had predicted, the lower portion of the youngest of their four children was protruding from beneath the hood of an ancient Dodge Charger.

Barbara gave the blue-jeaned rump a friendly swat.

"Hey, hon, can you haul yourself out of your favorite playground? There's something bothering me, and I'd like to talk about it."

"Sure, Mom. Hang loose for a sec, and I'll be right with you."

There were some clanking sounds as an unseen tool struck repeatedly against something metallic. Then Jamie came inching out from under the car hood, disheveled and plastered with grease but looking triumphant.

"I think I may finally have figured out what the problem is. And Brad was so sure I'd never get this running!"

"It's Brad I want to talk to you about," said Barbara. "I can't get that phone call from him out of my mind."

"I'm sure he feels bad about waking you up like that."

"That's not what worries me," said Barbara. "It was the way he *sounded*. His voice—he was all worked up. You know, almost hyper. He didn't sound like someone who'd spent the day fishing."

"You don't know how excited Brad gets when he's had a good catch," said Jamie.

"Yes, but, still . . ." She hesitated, trying to decide how to pave the way for the question she had come out to the garage to ask. Knowing how defensive Jamie always was about Brad, she feared that no matter how she phrased it, it would be considered an unforgivable accusation.

"You know how fond I am of Brad," she began tentatively. "He's been in and out of our house for so many years, I've come to feel that he's almost an extra son."

"What are you getting at, Mom?" Jamie asked suspiciously.

"It's because I love Brad that I'm worried about him," said Barbara. She drew a long breath and took the plunge. "Brad isn't acting normal these days. I think he ought to be getting some counseling. It's as though he isn't living in the same world with the rest of us."

As she had anticipated, Jamie became immediately hostile.

"You *know* how much stuff has gone wrong for him in the past few years! First, out of the blue, his father drops dead of a heart attack. Then his mother marries a guy Brad can't stand. They get a divorce, and that awful thing happens to Mindy. Isn't that enough to make anybody spacey?"

"From the things Laura Brummer's told me, 'spacey' is an understatement," Barbara said. "She says Brad won't even let her give Mindy's clothes away. And he won't let her take down the high chair. He wants it kept at the table, as though that baby were still there to sit in it."

"Brad's mother's got no right to pass judgment!" snapped Jamie. "She's an emotional mess herself and always has been!"

"Granted, Laura's unstable. Still, she isn't crazy. She's managed to accept what's happened to Mindy, and Brad hasn't."

"Are you trying to say *Brad* is crazy?"

"No, of course not. You don't have to be crazy to crack under pressure. It seems to me Brad is looking at life in a twisted way. What I'm worried about is that he might lose all touch with reality."

"Just because he called here later at night than he should have? It's natural to lose track of time when you're up in the mountains."

"I don't think Brad *was* in the mountains," said Barbara. "I do think he was calling long distance—I could hear the hum on the line—but I don't believe he was calling from the Pecos. He said he was phoning from a twenty-four-hour convenience store. There isn't any such store in the village of Terrero."

"How do you know there isn't?"

"I asked your father. If you'll remember, he was up there last fall during deer hunting season. He says there's a grocery store and a gas station, and they both close at six." She paused, waiting for Jamie's reaction. When there was none, she continued, "Where is he really? The two of you always tell each other everything. He must have filled you in on where he was going."

"What he told me was just what he told you on the telephone," said Jamie. "He said he was going up to his dad's old cabin. He said he needed to get away by himself for a while, and he'd be back for school next Monday."

"Was there anything else he told you?" Barbara prodded. "Believe me, dear, I'm not trying to stir up problems. I'm concerned that Brad may be in trouble. I know how loyal you are to him, and I hate to ask you to break a confidence, but I really do think it's important for you to tell me."

The silence that followed this statement seemed interminable. Then, just as she was beginning to think no answer would be forthcoming, Jamie suddenly blurted, "A couple of weeks ago . . ."

The sentence hung there between them, aching for completion.

"What happened a couple of weeks ago?" Barbara asked gently.

"Brad asked me if I'd go with him to help find Mindy. He said he thought Gavin had taken her to Texas."

"He wanted you to help find Mindy!" Barbara struggled to keep the horror out of her voice. "Brad asked you to do *that*, and you didn't tell his mother!"

"How could I?" Jamie responded. "You know she couldn't handle it."

"You don't have a choice. You've *got* to go over there and tell her tomorrow. Dear Lord, now I really *am* sure there's something wrong with Brad!"

She braced herself for a hot denial.

Instead, Jamie said miserably, "So am I, Mom."

Chapter 13

They had been driving for over an hour in total silence.

Tracy sat with her head resting against the back of the seat, watching the highway unwind in front of them in the beam of their headlights like a strand of thread from a swiftly rolling spool. The lights of approaching cars struck her eyes and fell away again at irregular intervals, becoming less frequent the farther they got from Winfield. On either side of the car lay great masses of darkness, broken only occasionally by a flicker of lamplight from the window of a distant farmhouse.

She was surprised to find herself feeling relaxed and drowsy, the way she usually felt after final exams. She had done what she had to do, and the challenge was over. It was behind her now, and the outcome was out of her hands.

"What will happen when we get there?" she asked idly.

She was not particularly worried, merely curious.

"We'll celebrate," Brad said without taking his eyes from the road.

"Celebrate how?"

"You get to choose. You're the heroine of the day. Everybody has their own idea of what a celebration is. I know a lot of kids who go out and get stoned, but I'm not much into that sort of thing myself. Jamie and I like to celebrate the big occasions in our lives by binging on chocolate mint ice cream."

"You're always talking about Jamie," Tracy commented. "You must be awfully good friends."

"Jamie and I go back a long way," said Brad. "We got to be buddies back in fourth grade. The two of you are alike in a lot of ways. Jamie would have thought about packing up Mindy's clothes. That's the kind of thing that would never have occurred to me."

"So, when we get to Albuquerque, you and Jamie and I will eat ice cream. What happens after that? I mean, what happens to *me?*"

"You'll bite the bullet and call your aunt, I guess. You're going to have to let her know where you are."

"Uncle Cory will blow his stack when I don't come home tonight," said Tracy. "There's no way I'll ever be able to go back there now."

"You won't have to go back," Brad said. "You can stay with us."

"You mean, *live* with you? Oh, come *on* now! What would your mother say?"

"She'll be happy to have you," said Brad. "Mom hates to be alone. If you're there with her I won't feel so guilty about leaving to go off to college."

"You make it sound so simple."

"It *will* be simple."

"Nothing you think will be simple ever really is."

"Don't worry," Brad said reassuringly. "Everything is going to be great. We've got Mindy, we're headed for home—we've got it *made.*"

Once again they fell into a companionable silence. The only sound in the car was the hiss of wind racing past the open windows. The sweet, rich smells of the countryside washed against Tracy's face, filling her nostrils with the fragrance of grass and earth and flowers and running water.

After a time Brad opened the glove compartment and extracted a cassette, which he inserted into the tape player on the dashboard. The voice of Barry Manilow came on at low volume. "I write the songs," he sang, "I write the songs."

The tiny slice of moon that Tracy had seen last through the window in the Carvers' kitchen had now climbed to the peak of the sky, where it hung suspended from the edge of a tattered cloud. The words of the lullaby on the tape recorder in Mindy's bedroom drifted back into her mind: *The moon is wise, the moon is old, and all her songs come wrapped in gold.* The moon in the sky tonight was far from gold; it was pearly and iridescent, a moon to be wished on.

She tried to think of something wonderful to wish for and found she was too exhausted to make the effort.

Would it truly work out? she asked herself, letting her eyes fall closed. Would she be able to build a life with Brad and his family? The idea of living with strangers was oddly appealing, like starting over again with a whole new identity. When she had gone to live with her aunt and uncle, her former life had gone with her. Every time she gazed into her aunt's face, she had seen a distorted version of the mother she had lost. To leave all the pain behind her and become another person would be so much easier than having to deal with the remnants of her former existence.

She wondered what Brad would be like on his own turf. Would their relationship be that of brother and sister? At their first meeting, he had given her the impression that he was attracted to her, but that might have been only because he needed her to help him. In the past few days he had treated her like a trusted but platonic partner, not like a girl in whom he had a romantic interest.

"What's Albuquerque like?" she asked him now, more to make conversation than because it mattered.

"It's a nice place to live," Brad said. "It's a good-sized city with a lot going on, but it's located in a sort of a bowl that's surrounded by mountains. You can drive up into the forest area, and in only about twenty minutes you feel like you're a million miles from anywhere."

"The closest thing to mountains I've ever seen were high-rise office buildings," said Tracy. "It's hard to picture the sort of place you're describing."

"It's more beautiful than anything you could ever imagine," said Brad. "The best times I ever had in my life were the weekends my dad and I spent up in the mountains. Dad bought some land in the Pecos with a cabin already on it, and he and I worked together to fix it up. We'd go up there in the spring and summer to fish, and in the fall we'd make it our base for hunting trips."

"Since your father died, do you still spend time there?" asked Tracy.

"I used to, back when Mom was first married to Gavin. There was all the lovey-dovey, newlywed stuff going on at home, and Mom didn't seem to care if I was there or not. Later on, when the bloom was off and they started having arguments, she wanted me around for moral support. Since the divorce, I haven't been up to the cabin once. I miss the place. It's more home to me than our house in town."

"I guess it must bring back a lot of happy memories."

"Yes, everything about it reminds me of Dad. When I wake up there in the mornings I lie in my bunk and listen to the sound of the stream rushing by outside the window, and I picture Dad out there in his boots and waders. Sometimes I even think I can hear his footsteps on the porch. I feel like any minute he might start yelling, 'Get up, you lazy kid! We've got trout for breakfast!' "

He paused and then asked, "What do you remember best about your mom? Was there some special place you used to go together?"

"To the theater," Tracy responded immediately. "We spent a lot of time at the theater. And at art galleries. The Metropolitan Museum of Art was right on the subway route, and we used to go there on Sunday afternoons. And Central Park—as a kid I used to love to go there. It's like a big green island in the middle of the city, with playgrounds and flowers and paths and a little lake. We used to make boats out of paper cups and put sails on them, and when it was breezy we'd take them to the park and race them."

"You and your mother?"

She hesitated and then said, "No."

It surprised her to recall it had been her *father* who had sailed boats with her. Richard Lloyd had been the one who had knelt beside her at the edge of the lake and sent a fleet of Dixie cups out to face the waves. It was he who had pushed her on swings so she soared high above the earth, like a bird who was taking flight into the bright summer sky. It was he who had carried her piggyback along flower-bordered paths and had plucked a petunia and tucked it behind her ear.

During her early years she had loved her parents equally. They had seemed so special, the two of them, handsomer and brighter than other children's parents— like a god and goddess, too good for the world they lived in.

Her mother had told her how she'd hated growing up in Winfield. "The instant I graduated, I took off for New York," she had said. "I had talent and looks and a dream of becoming an actress, and I wasn't going to let anything stop me from making it. Your Aunt Rene and I are as different as a plow horse and a racehorse. Rene was happy to stay in Winfield and look after our parents. After they died, she married Cory, who had been her boyfriend in high school and had gone on to business school to become an accountant. I don't imagine their marriage is the world's most romantic love match, but I'm sure the two of them have a lot in common."

The sway of the car and the drone of Manilow's voice were a hypnotic combination. Tracy did not mean to fall asleep and did not realize that she had done so until she opened her eyes to see that the moon was gone. When she brought her head forward she saw it resting on the edge of the horizon like a beached canoe and noticed the sky behind it was lighter than it had been.

The car felt somehow different. The road seemed rougher. She realized it had been the jolting sensation that had wakened her. "What's happened?" she asked. "Are we still on the highway?"

"No," Brad told her. "There was a roadblock at the state border a few miles south of here. When I saw it up ahead I turned off onto a side road. I thought I'd go north on that for a while and then try to find another road leading west."

"They were probably just making an insurance check," said Tracy. "Gavin would never have had the nerve to call the police. What on earth would he have told them? 'A baby I kidnapped has been taken back by her brother'?"

"I don't think he'd do that either," Brad agreed. "The Carvers might, though. For all we know, Gavin may have told them he's the custodial parent. If that's the case, they could think *we're* the ones who are pulling a child-snatch —either that or that Mindy has been kidnapped by strangers."

As though in response to her name, the child in the back seat spoke.

"Mommy?" she murmured drowsily.

"Go back to sleep, baby," Brad told her. "We haven't gotten home yet. You're going to see your mommy in a couple of hours."

"I wet," Mindy announced in a pathetic voice.

"Oh, no!" Tracy exclaimed, suddenly guilty. "I forgot I was supposed to have taken her to the bathroom."

"We'd better stop here, then, and get her changed," said Brad. "We can't let her stay in wet pants all the way to Albuquerque."

He pulled the car over to the side of the road and brought it to a stop. When he opened the door to get out, the ceiling light popped on, illuminating the car's interior. Tracy turned to glance behind her and saw that the child was sitting upright, still holding her monkey.

Her face was flushed from sleep, and her eyes were frightened. She blinked at the flood of light and started to whimper.

Brad opened the rear door and leaned in to smile at her.

"Hi, Mindy," he said gently. "Remember me?"

Mindy jerked away from him and began to cry in earnest.

"Mommy!" she wailed. "Want Mommy!"

"She doesn't seem to recognize you," said Tracy.

At the sound of a female voice, Mindy stretched out her arms imploringly.

"I wet!" she sobbed.

"You'd better come back here and change her, Tracy," Brad said. "She's so worked up she's not going to let me touch her."

Tracy got out of the car and stepped onto the shoulder of the road. A thick growth of ragged weeds felt like clusters of wire against the calves of her legs as she went around to take Brad's place at the rear door.

Mindy's hopeful expression vanished when she caught sight of her.

"You not Mommy!" she said.

"It's all right," Tracy told her soothingly. "I'm your baby-sitter. Your Aunt Sally must have told you a sitter was going to be staying with you tonight while she and your Uncle Doug went out to dinner. My name's Tracy, and we're going for a little ride."

"A ride?" Mindy repeated, glancing about her. Obviously she had not realized she was in a car.

Tracy got into the back seat and held out her arms. Too limp with sleep to resist this offer of comfort, Mindy let herself be drawn close and cuddled. The odor of urine was all but overwhelming. The little girl's pajama bottoms were soaking.

Pressing the child gently back onto the blanket, Tracy pulled the wet clothing off her and dropped it onto the floor. Then she rummaged through the contents of one of the sacks in search of dry pants.

Brad shut the rear door and climbed back into the driver's seat. He raised his hand and adjusted the switch so the ceiling light would remain on once the car doors were closed. Then he turned the key in the ignition and started the engine. "We might as well get back on the road while you change her clothes," he said. "We've still got a good way to go, and it's best to keep moving."

Digging down in the bag, Tracy finally located a second pair of pajama bottoms. "Whose are these?" she asked, holding them up so the child could see them. "Do these Smurf pajamas belong to Mindy?"

"No," Mindy said. "Those jammies Cricket's."

"Cricket's your nickname," said Tracy. "Mindy's your

real name. Don't you remember how everybody used to call you Mindy?"

"Juicy Yan," said Mindy. "Cricket Juicy Yan."

"Juicy?" Tracy repeated in bewilderment. "Like Juicy Fruit gum?"

"Cricket," Mindy said firmly. "Cricket's jammies."

"All right, you can be Cricket if you like that better," Tracy said. "How about giving me some help putting Cricket's pajamas on?"

The child obligingly thrust her feet into the air to allow the dry pants to be slipped up over her ankles. The car was going too fast for the road it was traveling. It kept dipping in and out of potholes, making it hard to accomplish anything that required coordination.

With difficulty, Tracy managed to work the pajamas past the child's damp buttocks and slide them up around her waist. She was in the process of adjusting the waistband when suddenly she froze.

Slowly, she drew the elastic away from Mindy's stomach.

"Brad," she said, "didn't you tell me Gavin once burned her?"

"Back when she was a toddler," Brad said, nodding. "He was working on his car stereo with a soldering iron. He forgot she was out there with him and burned her belly."

"Was it a serious burn?"

"Bad enough," Brad said. "She didn't have to have skin grafts or anything like that, but when she grows up she won't want to wear a bikini." He adjusted the rearview mirror so he could look back at them. "Why are you asking that? Oh, I see—you're looking at the scar."

"Mindy doesn't have any scar," said Tracy.

Chapter 14

"Are you blind?" exclaimed Brad. "Of course, there's a scar!"

"No, there isn't," said Tracy, staring down at the smooth, unblemished skin of the child's pink abdomen. "There's not a mark on her, Brad."

"That's impossible," Brad said. He was silent a moment. Then he said, "Maybe Gavin had it removed. He knew it was something we could use to have her identified. If his plan was to start all over, changing her name and disguising her history, then it would make sense that he would have gotten rid of the scar."

"You can't just wipe away a scar as though it never existed," Tracy protested. "At least, not when it's from a burn like the one you described. Mindy's stomach is perfect. There's not even a scratch."

"This light's too poor to see anything much," said Brad. "Or it might just be the scar has faded. That could have happened. Maybe it wasn't as bad as it seemed at first."

"Or, maybe . . ." Tracy began, and left the sentence dangling. The idea that had slipped into her mind for one terrible second was so outrageous that she would not even allow herself to put it into words.

Brad reached up and flicked off the ceiling light, and once again the world within the car was plunged into darkness. Mindy gave a sigh and burrowed her head into Tracy's side as though it were a pillow, twisting and turning until she found a comfortable position on the seat and then making a nest there. Once she had settled herself into place, it was only a matter of minutes before her body went limp and her breathing grew deep and steady.

Tracy was too wide awake to contemplate sleeping again. Holding herself as still as possible so as not to disturb the child, she sat gazing out through the side window into the night. Eventually the sky in the east began to grow lighter, and a thin strip of pink appeared along the horizon. As the blackness lessened, flat fields studded with what appeared to be boulders gradually materialized on either side of the car. Then in one magical instant the sky exploded into crimson, and the hulking shapes proved to be cattle, standing motionless, with their heads buried deep in grass as though they were ostriches.

Brad continued to drive north along the rutted road for another half hour, at which time it intersected with a two-lane-blacktop road, and he was able to turn west again.

By now the sun was gold and the sky was blue, and dawn had given way to full-fledged morning. The first sign of human life was a Texaco station perched on the edge of a cornfield.

"That's a beautiful sight," Brad said when he caught his first glimpse of it. "We've been running with our gauge on empty for the past five miles."

He pulled into the station in front of a self-serve gas pump, switched off the engine, and climbed out of the car. Easing Mindy down onto the seat so she was no longer propped against her, Tracy opened the rear door and got out also.

"I'll be back in a minute," she told Brad. "I need to find a rest room."

Inside the gas station, an attendant in olive green coveralls sat dozing behind the cash register. A portable radio on the counter next to him was spouting forth the morning news.

"Could I please have the key to the ladies' room?" Tracy asked him.

"It's on the wall by the Coke machine," the man informed her. "The bathrooms are around at the back. You have to go outside to get to them."

The keys to the rest rooms were attached to blocks of wood, one of which was marked with an *S* and the other with an *F*. Reasoning that whatever the "S" stood for, *F* must stand for *female*, Tracy took that key down from the nail on which it was hanging and was preparing to leave the office when the voice of the radio announcer spoke the name *Carver*.

It struck her like a fist driven into her stomach. Her breath went out of her with an audible gasp, and she found herself struggling frantically to refill her lungs.

". . . a light blue Chevrolet Impala with New Mexico license plates," the newscaster continued as a windup to his report. "On a happier note, the weather today will be . . ."

"Are you all right, miss?" asked the man at the register.

"Yes, thank you," Tracy managed to tell him. "Yes, I'm just fine."

With more effort than she had ever had to make before to do anything, she forced herself to walk out through the open door into the sun-jeweled morning.

Circling the building, she came to two doors, one marked STALLIONS and the other FILLIES. She unlocked the latter, pushed it open, and stepped inside. The dank little room was foul with mildew and disinfectant, and the damp floor sucked at Tracy's shoes like a hungry blotter. The walls were covered with graffiti, and on the door to the toilet stall someone had used purple lipstick to make an obscene drawing.

Tracy used the toilet and then washed her hands at the rust-stained sink. She went through the motions mechanically, barely conscious of what she was doing. In the mirror over the basin the ashen oval of her face looked as though it belonged to someone who was deathly ill.

A light blue Chevrolet Impala . . . She lathered her palms with thick yellow slime from the soap dispenser and held them under the cold stream of water from the spigot. Her hands were shaking, and her fingernails made little clicking sounds against the porcelain. . . . *New Mexico license plates* . . .

Her soul felt as icy as the water.

She turned off the faucet and dried her hands on a paper towel. Then she went back to the office to return the key. The attendant was fully awake now; he was munching on a chocolate bar and counting the bills in the register. Either he had switched stations or the news program had come to an end, for the radio was playing country-western music.

When she returned to the car she found that Brad was now on the passenger side. He motioned for her to get into the driver's seat.

"I think you'd better take over for a while," he said. "If I don't get a nap, I'm going to fall asleep at the wheel."

Tracy got into the car, but she made no attempt to start it.

"Brad, they *know*," she said shakily. "Gavin must have called the police after all. Either that or the Carvers did. I just heard the end of a radio newscast. The announcer was describing our car."

"It's lucky we got off the highway then," said Brad. "That must have been the reason for the roadblock."

"He said it had New Mexico license plates. How can they know that? Doug Carver couldn't have read that plate without a flashlight."

"The next-door neighbor probably told them," Brad said. "She got a good look at the car the other morning. Get a grip on yourself, Tracy. So what if they know we have Mindy? We haven't done anything wrong. Mindy's my *sister*."

"Yes, I know," Tracy said, beginning to feel a bit foolish. "It was a shock, that's all. Hearing the name 'Carver' leap out from nowhere the way it did, having our car described as though we were criminals running from the law—"

"Put it out of your mind," Brad said. "There's nothing to worry about. We've already crossed the border into New Mexico, and this road will take us most of the way into Albuquerque. I'm going to catch an hour's worth of shut-eye. Wake me up when you see a place to stop for breakfast."

We haven't done anything wrong, Tracy reassured herself, grasping at the statement and clutching it to her. Brad's lack of concern was not sufficient to quell her own, however. When enough time had passed so she was certain he was fully asleep, she reached over and pressed the button to eject the cassette he had put in the tape player. Then she turned on the radio and adjusted the dial until she found a Texas station that was broadcasting news.

Keeping the volume turned low, she listened to accounts of the newest crisis in the Middle East, of a bomb threat at Miami Airport, and then, in gentle contrast, the news that the residents of western Texas could expect a weekend of "clear skies, rising winds in the late afternoon, and temperatures in the mid to low seventies."

At the program's end, there came the story for which she had been waiting, but the content was not at all what she had been prepared for.

"Three-year-old Julianne Carver of Winfield, Texas, was kidnapped last night by her teenage baby-sitter," the announcer said briskly. "The child's father, Douglas Carver, said he was forced at gunpoint into a kitchen storage room, where he was held captive while the sitter and a male accomplice abducted his daughter. Warrants have been issued for the arrest of Tracy Lloyd, age seventeen, five foot six, one hundred fifteen pounds, brown hair and blue eyes, and an unidentified teenage boy, approximately five foot seven, with brown curly hair. The pair is presumed to be traveling in a blue Chevrolet Impala with New Mexico license plates. They are armed and considered dangerous."

The shock hit Tracy with such velocity that her head was filled with a roar like the sound of rushing wind. The length of road ahead of her dissolved into mist, and the car lurched out of control, swinging wildly over to the far side of the left lane. Dizziness struck her, and for one terrifying moment she thought she was going to lose consciousness. Then the frantic blast of a car horn jerked her back to reality. Gripping the steering wheel with all her strength, she gave it a desperate twist, bringing the car back onto the right side of the road just in time to avoid a head-on collision with a pickup truck.

Clutching the wheel with white-knuckled hands, as a drowning person might cling to a life preserver, she glanced across at Brad in the seat beside her. To her amazement, he was still sleeping soundly.

In the rearview mirror, however, she could see that the child in the back seat was sitting up.

"Julianne?" Tracy asked her softly. "Is your name *Julianne?*"

The child in the mirror regarded her without responding.

"Cricket?" Tracy tried again. "Is Cricket's real name Julianne Carver?"

After a moment, the blond head nodded.

"Cricket's big name Juicy Yan," the little girl acknowledged. "Where's Mommy? I want Mommy!"

"Your Mommy's at home," Tracy told her, struggling to keep her voice steady. "I'm going to get you back to her right away."

She continued to drive. The road was back in focus now. She was able to see and hear, and also to think. The thoughts that churned in her brain were a bewildering jumble, none of them leading to anything that made any sense. The incredible possibility that had occurred to her for one fleeting instant when she had discovered that the child in their car did not have a scar had suddenly become a horrifying reality.

The little girl was not Mindy Brummer! If the radio report was true—and there was no reason to believe that it was not—she was the daughter, not the niece, of Doug and Sally Carver. Why had Brad pretended Cricket was his sister? Did he even *have* a sister, and if so, where was she? Had he invented the entire story of a child-snatching stepfather in order to manipulate Tracy into participating in a kidnapping? If that was indeed the case, then what was his motive? Could he be thinking of holding the child for ransom? And how did Gavin Brummer fit into the picture? Why had both he and Brad been carrying identical photographs of a child who was not even a member of their immediate family?

The world around them was now awake and in motion. They passed a boy on a bicycle delivering newspapers and a girl in blue jeans feeding a flock of geese. In a yard in front of a farmhouse, several young children dressed in pajamas were climbing down from a tree house, and a woman with her hair in curlers was watering a garden plot.

Ten miles farther down the road, they entered a village. Tracy reduced speed as she drove through the tiny business district and pulled to a stop at a traffic light at the end of the first block. There was a café on the corner directly across from them, and the smell of freshly baked cinnamon rolls wafted in through the car's open window.

"Hungry!" Cricket announced suddenly. "I want breffuss!"

Awakened either by the decrease in speed or by the child's shrill statement, Brad opened his eyes and straightened up in his seat.

"Breakfast," he echoed sleepily, rubbing his eyes. "That sounds good to me too. Where are we, anyway?"

"This is Rock Springs," Tracy told him. "There was a sign at the town limits."

She was amazed at how calm and natural her voice sounded.

"Great!" Brad said. "That means we're only a couple of hours from Albuquerque. What do you say we stop here and eat? Mindy says she's hungry, and I didn't get a chance to get dinner last night."

The parking area next to Maria's Café was empty except for an ancient Plymouth and a pair of motorcycles. Tracy parked the car next to the Plymouth and got out. The soreness of her arms and shoulders attested to the fact that she had been driving with her muscles knotted up with tension, and it was all she could do to straighten her fingers after the hour they had spent in a frozen grip on the steering wheel.

Brad got out on the passenger side and opened the rear door of the car for Cricket.

"Let's go, Mindy," he said. "We're going to go eat now."

Regarding him with obvious distrust, the child made no effort to move.

"*Cricket,*" she said defiantly.

"Your name's Mindy," Brad corrected her. "You can't have forgotten that. Cricket's just a silly nickname. Put that monkey down, and let's go inside and eat."

The little girl glanced from Brad to Tracy and back to Brad again. Her eyes filled with tears, and her lower lip began to quiver.

"Juicy Yan Cricket," she insisted. "Monk-Monk's hungry."

"It's okay, Cricket," Tracy said gently. "Let me help you get your shoes on. You can bring Monk-Monk in for breakfast, too, if you want to."

"Don't call her by that dumb name," Brad objected. "She's got to get used to being Mindy again. And the minute we get back to Albuquerque I'm buying her another Bimbo, and that ugly toy monkey goes into the garbage can."

The door of Maria's Café opened into a tiny entrance hall where a cash register and a postcard rack were located. Beyond that, through a wide double door, lay the dining area. As the dearth of cars in the parking lot had indicated, the coffee shop was virtually empty of customers. Two young men in black windbreakers sat at a table by the front window, and an elderly man, seated alone at another table, was engrossed in reading a newspaper. The remainder of the tables were unoccupied.

Brad led the way to a booth at the back of the room and settled Cricket on the seat beside him. He picked up the menu and studied it for a moment. "I think I'm going to have French toast," he said. "Mindy's going to want that, too, aren't you, baby?"

The child shook her head. "Cricket wants Froot Loops."

"Cereal?" Brad exclaimed. "French toast is your favorite thing! That's what Mommy always makes you for special breakfasts."

"No, Froot Loops," Cricket insisted. "Froot Loops! Froot Loops!"

"Okay, Froot Loops it is," Brad said. "What do you want, Tracy?"

"I don't care," said Tracy. "You order for me. What I need to do now is locate a rest room."

"Again?" Brad regarded her quizzically.

"Yes, again."

Without further comment, she got up from the table and went back out to the entrance hall. A sign on the wall behind the register indicated that the rest rooms were located down a short hall to the right. Hoping that Brad was too preoccupied with ordering breakfast to be watching her through the doorway, Tracy turned instead to the left, and crossed quickly over to the pay phone in the corner.

Once the receiver was in her hand and she had dropped a quarter into the coin slot, she suddenly realized that she did not know whom to call. The last thing she wanted to do was talk to the Carvers, at least until she could give a reason for their child's abduction. She had no idea why Brad had taken their daughter; all she knew about him was what he had chosen to tell her. She could not even be sure that his name *was* Brad Johnson, since she had never insisted on seeing identification. As things now stood, the boy she knew as Brad was in a position to walk out the door and disappear from her life at the first opportunity, leaving her with a kidnapped child in her possession and no explanation to offer as to why she had been taken.

Too much time was passing. Brad would be wondering what was keeping her. This might well be her final opportunity to put through a phone call. She had no guarantee they were really headed for Albuquerque or that Brad had a mother there who would be happy to see them. Once they were back in the car and he was again behind the wheel, she might never have another chance to make contact with anyone.

Making a hasty decision, she dialed information.

"I need a number in Albuquerque," she said. "The person's name is Brummer, Mrs. Gavin Brummer."

There was a pause while the operator checked the listings.

Then she said, "I don't have a listing for Gavin Brummer, but I do have one for a Laura Brummer on Locust Street."

"That could be the one," Tracy said. "Can you give me the number?"

She jotted it down on the edge of the telephone directory and dialed it as soon as the operator was off the line.

The phone was answered by a woman's voice, and the operator came on the line again, asking for money.

Tracy fumbled in her wallet for coins and fed them into the slot without bothering to count them.

"Hello," she said. "I'm not sure I'm calling the right number. I'm trying to reach a Mrs. Brummer who has a son named Brad Johnson."

"I'm Brad's mother," the woman said immediately. "What's happened? Has there been an accident?"

"No, Brad's fine," said Tracy. "The one I'm calling about is Mindy. You do have a little girl named Mindy, don't you?"

The silence that followed was longer than it should

have been, considering the question required a one-word answer.

When Laura Brummer did speak again, her voice was flat and expressionless.

"My daughter was killed four months ago," she said.

Chapter 15

She was *killed!*" Tracy repeated, unable to believe what she had heard.

"Four months ago," Laura Brummer said again. "Last December, on her second birthday, my precious baby was run over by a car."

"I'm so sorry," Tracy gasped, at a loss for words. "Brad told me—I mean, he really seems to believe she was kidnapped by her father!"

"Brad believes what he wants to believe," Brad's mother said tersely. "The way my psychologist tried to explain it to me, my son's way of coping with pain is by denial. Who are you, and how do you know Brad?"

"My name's Tracy Lloyd," said Tracy. "I met Brad this past week in Winfield, Texas."

"You met him *where*?" Laura Brummer sounded startled. "Brad told me he was going camping. He said he was going to be up in the Pecos, fishing."

"He drove to Texas to look for his sister," said Tracy. "He asked me if I'd help him, and I agreed. We found this blond little girl Brad told me was Mindy, and I managed to get myself hired as her baby-sitter." She drew a long breath and forced herself to plunge ahead. "We *took* her."

"You took her? You don't mean to tell me you've *kidnapped* some strange child!"

"Brad told me the child was Mindy," Tracy said miserably. "I've just discovered her name is Julianne Carver."

"Brad has *Cricket!*" Laura Brummer exclaimed incredulously. "That's my ex-husband's niece! Do you have her with you now? Where in heaven's name *are* you?"

"Yes, she's here with us," said Tracy. "We're in Rock Springs, New Mexico, at a place called Maria's Café."

"Why, you're only a couple of hours from Albuquerque!" said Brad's mother. "Where are you taking Cricket? Are you bringing her here?"

"I don't know," said Tracy. "That's what Brad's been saying, but then he's told me so many things that have turned out not to be true that I don't know what to believe anymore."

"You mustn't let him take off again!" Laura Brummer exclaimed. "I'll have somebody come out there right away to get you. I'd do it myself, but I'm too upset to drive safely. Brad's friend Jamie is here now. Let me check and see"—her voice grew muffled as she turned away from the phone—"Jamie, can you drive to Rock Springs and pick up Brad? Oh, thank goodness! I knew I could count on you, dear." She spoke into the receiver again. "Brad's been so disturbed lately, Jamie's the only one these days who can really get through to him. You make sure he doesn't leave before Jamie gets there."

"How can I hold him here if he doesn't want to stay?"

"You'll have to figure out something," Brad's mother said helplessly. "I'll call Gavin and ask him to deal with the Carvers. If they know their child is unharmed and will soon be returned to them, maybe they can be persuaded not to press charges. I simply can't believe this! What a nightmare!"

At that point, the operator came back on the line to ask Tracy to deposit more money. Since she had already emptied her coin purse, the conversation ended abruptly, with Mrs. Brummer's assurance that Jamie Hanson would leave for Rock Springs immediately.

After she had hung up the receiver, Tracy continued to stand by the telephone, unsure about what it was she ought to do next. All the possibilities that leapt into her mind were ridiculous: ordering something exotic that would take a long time to prepare and then dawdling over breakfast; taking Cricket into the ladies' room and setting up residence there where Brad couldn't get at them; finding some way to confiscate Brad's wallet so he would be unable to pay their bill and would not be allowed to leave the restaurant.

Conscious that she was in a state of mental hysteria, she made a concentrated effort to focus her mind upon more realistic alternatives. After a moment, she realized it had to be the car. Brad's car was the only means of transportation they had. If she could manage to put the Chevy out of commission, they would be stuck in Rock Springs until it could be repaired.

But how did one go about sabotaging an automobile? She knew next to nothing about a car's inner workings. With so many parts that could be tampered with, there had to be some simple way of making one inoperable. Maybe she could slash the tires or put water in the gas tank. Or perhaps she could simply open the hood and disconnect all the wires she saw, twisting them into such a tangle that sorting them out and reattaching them would take hours.

Tracy glanced at her watch. Twelve minutes had passed since she had left the dining room. If she didn't return by the time the food arrived at the table, it was very probable Brad would come looking for her.

Whatever she ended up doing would have to be done quickly. Ignoring the curious glance of the girl behind the cash register, she opened the door and went back outside. Ducking as she passed the front window so as to avoid being seen by the occupants of the dining room, she hurried around the side of the building and entered the parking lot in which they had left the car. The vehicles that had been in the lot when they had arrived there were just as they had been, but the space next to the Plymouth was empty.

Brad's Chevy was gone.

For a long moment, Tracy stood staring at the vacant spot where the car had been. Were Brad's delusions contagious? Had she, too, lost her senses? Had they really parked in this spot, and, if so, where was the car?

Slowly, she walked over to the Plymouth and placed the flat of her hand against one of its dented fenders. The feel of the sun-warmed metal beneath her palm renewed her sense of reality. She was not hallucinating, nor was she dreaming. There could be only one rational explanation for the car's disappearance. The obvious answer, of course, was that it had been stolen.

The incredible coincidence of having such an improbable event occur at this particular time and place was so beyond belief that it was all she could do to accept the fact that it had happened. Then, it suddenly struck her that this solved her problem! She would not have to take any further steps to prevent Brad from leaving Rock Springs. He had no way of taking them anywhere until somebody came from Albuquerque to collect them.

Her relief was so great, she felt as though she had been administered a tranquilizing drug. Leaving the lot, she completed her circle of the building and reentered the restaurant. Once inside, she headed directly for the dining room and started back toward the booth where she had left Brad and Cricket.

Her view of the table was blocked by a waitress with a tray. It was not until Tracy had reached the table that the girl stepped aside to reveal the fact that, rather than serving food as Tracy had assumed she was doing, she was actually in the process of clearing away uneaten breakfasts—two plates of French toast, a bowl of cereal, and several glasses of juice and mugs of coffee.

The booth itself was empty.

The moment of shock that Tracy had experienced in the parking lot was minor in comparison with what she felt now. "What do you think you're doing?" she asked.

"Oh, I'm sorry!" the waitress exclaimed, glancing up in surprise. "I thought you'd left with the others."

"Where are the people who were sitting here?" Tracy asked her.

"The young man and the little girl left about five minutes ago. I thought you were all one party and you were leaving with them. I'll have your plate reheated for you right away."

"I *was* part of their party," said Tracy. "I didn't expect them to leave like this. Did the boy say anything to indicate where they were going?"

The waitress shook her head.

"I thought it seemed pretty strange, ordering all this food and then nobody staying to eat it. I brought it in, and the young man got up and went over to the doorway as though he were looking for somebody out in the hall. He stood there a minute and then came back and put some money on the table. Then he and the little girl went out the back way, through the kitchen. I thought you must have gone out to the car and they were meeting you there."

"I see," Tracy said.

She *did* see, all too well.

"Don't you want to sit down and—"

"No, thank you. Not right now."

Gripping the edge of the table, Tracy made a violent effort not to give way to the wave of faintness that was threatening to overpower her. She had the horrible feeling that if she allowed herself to sit down her legs might turn to rubber and she would never again get up.

After a moment, she turned and went back out to the entrance hall. She crossed to the desk and took a dollar bill out of her wallet. "I need some change," she said to the cashier. "I have to make another call."

Back at the telephone, she went momentarily blank on Laura Brummer's number, until she remembered she had written it on the edge of the phone book. Dropping a coin into the slot, she dialed the necessary eleven digits. There was a pause and a click, and her ears were greeted by the impersonal staccato buzz of the busy signal.

When she hung up the receiver, there was a loud clink as her quarter fell through and came tumbling out into the dish beneath the coin return. Picking it up, Tracy held it, wondering what to do. She knew what her next call should be, and she dreaded the thought of it. Finally, bracing herself for the horrendous scene that was sure to be forthcoming, she dropped the quarter back into the slot and dialed zero.

The operator came on the line. "Can I help you?"

If only you could, Tracy thought. If only anyone could! Aloud, she said, "I want to place a collect call to Winfield, Texas."

This time, the phone did ring and was answered immediately.

"I have a collect call for anyone at this number from Tracy Lloyd," said the operator. "Will you accept the charges?"

"Of course!" Aunt Rene gave a gasp. "Tracy? Thank God, it's you! We've been so worried! Are you all right!"

"Yes," Tracy said. "I'm fine. I'm sorry I worried you."

"Where are you?"

"In New Mexico."

"Cory!" Her aunt's voice went momentarily distant as she turned away from the telephone. "Cory, it's Tracy! She's safe in New Mexico!" An instant later, she was back. "We've been worried sick, dear. What's happened? Is the little Carver girl with you?"

"She was, but she's not anymore," Tracy told her. "Brad has taken Cricket off somewhere in the car."

"Brad? You mean, the boy who broke into the Carvers' house was *Brad*? The way Doug Carver described him, we thought it was some maniac. Doug said a boy with a gun threatened to kill him. We've been out of our minds, we've been so frightened for your safety."

"I'm fine," Tracy said again. "And Cricket's fine too. No matter where he's taken her, I'm sure Brad won't hurt her. I heard on the radio there's a warrant out for our arrest."

"We tried to tell them you weren't involved," said Aunt Rene. "We knew you were taken by force, just the way the child was. Doug Carver wouldn't listen though. He insisted on telling the police you were part of it also. Nothing your uncle or I could say seemed to make a bit of difference to anybody."

"The police came to your house to get information about me?"

"They didn't have to come to our house," said Aunt Rene. "We were already at the Carvers' when Doug called them."

"I don't understand," said Tracy. "What were you doing *there*?"

"We drove over to see why the phone was off the

hook for so long. Nobody came to the door, so, since it wasn't locked, we went ahead and opened it. We could hear Doug Carver shouting from the pantry. The moment we got him out, he went straight to the phone and called his wife and then the police. Then Cory put through a call to your father in Italy."

"Uncle Cory phoned Dad!" Tracy exclaimed.

"Well, of course we had to phone Richard. You're his *daughter!* He was able to get himself booked on a morning flight out of Rome. He should be on his way back to the States this very minute."

"He couldn't take off like that! They're making a movie!"

"There was no way that poor man could work, knowing you were missing," said her aunt. "He was upset and frightened and, of course, furious at Cory and me. He entrusted you to our care, and we let this dreadful thing happen. For all we knew, you might have been raped or murdered!" Her aunt's voice faltered and then dissolved into a muffled sob.

The receiver gave a thud as though it had slipped from her hand, and a moment later Cory Stevenson's voice came on the line. "Where are you, Tracy? I'm coming to get you."

"That's not necessary," said Tracy. "Brad's mother has already sent somebody to pick us up. I don't know what's going to happen, though, when his friend arrives and finds out that Brad and Cricket aren't here any longer."

"I don't want you going off with anybody connected with that crazy Johnson kid," her uncle said firmly. "I want you home with us and out of this mess."

"I can't get 'out of this mess,'" Tracy said miserably. There was an obstruction in her throat that she could not force away. "I'm in it up to my neck."

"It's not your job to handle this. It's up to the police."

"I'm sorry," Tracy told him. "I'll call you soon, I promise. I feel terrible about having caused so many problems. I've got to do what I can, though, to help find Cricket. You may not want to believe this, Uncle Cory, but I'm as responsible for what's happened to her as Brad is."

She pressed down the cradle of the phone, breaking off their connection. Then she redeposited her quarter and once again dialed Laura Brummer's number.

This time the phone rang repeatedly without an answer.

Replacing the receiver, Tracy glanced down at her watch. It was slightly after 10 A.M. If Brad's mother had been correct in her estimate of the time it would take to drive to Rock Springs from Albuquerque, it would be at least 11:30 before Jamie arrived there. With that much time to kill, she could leave the restaurant and walk around town or pick up something to read. Still, there was always a chance that Brad might have a change of heart and decide to come back and get her. If that should occur, it was imperative that she should be there.

With that thought in mind, she went back into the café dining room, where she ordered coffee and a sweet roll and settled herself at a table to wait out the remainder of the morning.

Time had never seemed to pass so slowly. The men in the black jackets finished eating their pancakes and left. The man with the newspaper ordered himself more coffee, and a large Hispanic family came in and ordered ice cream. Their glossy-haired baby sat in a high chair and ate with his fingers, coating his round, dark-complected face with chocolate.

"Naughty boy!" said his mother. "Naughty Juanito!" She slapped his sticky hands, and Juanito howled.

You don't know how lucky you are, Tracy longed to

tell the woman. Your baby is alive and safe, and you know where he is.

The family eventually left, and the early lunch brigade began to arrive. Self-conscious about having stayed so long already, Tracy ordered a second sweet roll, which she did not want, and forced herself to take an occasional bite of it.

More time went by, and more people kept trickling in. Two overweight women in identical polyester pants suits, one lavender and one pink. A bearded man in boots and a cowboy hat. A gray-haired woman who walked with the aid of a cane. A teenage girl with an exquisite, high-cheekboned face, whose dark hair was pulled back and tied in a ponytail.

The girl did not move immediately to a table. Instead, she paused in the doorway and checked the room over as though she were expecting to find someone waiting there for her.

After a moment, she settled her gaze on Tracy and crossed the room to the table where she was sitting.

"You're the only girl here, so I guess you have to be Tracy," she said. "I'm Jamie Hanson, and I've come for Brad."

Chapter 16

Y ou're Jamie?" Tracy said blankly. "But Jamie's a boy!"

The girl looked surprised. "Brad told you *that*?"

"Actually, he didn't," Tracy admitted. "I just assumed —I mean, he kept talking about this person, Jamie, who was his best friend, so naturally, I thought—"

"He was right, I *am* his best friend," the girl said. "I always have been and always will be. So where is he?"

"I don't know," Tracy said.

"You don't know?" Now it was Jamie who appeared bewildered. "I was out at the Brummer house when you called there. There were some things my mom thought I should discuss with Brad's mother. I thought you told Mrs. Brummer Brad was with you!"

"At the time I called her, he was here in this dining room," Tracy said. "I had no reason to believe he wouldn't still be here when I got back from the telephone. When he wasn't, I tried to call his mother back. First the line was busy, and then there wasn't any answer."

"I dropped her off at my house," said Jamie. "She was pretty upset, and I didn't think she ought to be by herself. Gavin Brummer gave her hell when she told him it was Brad who had his sister's kid. Mrs. Brummer goes all to pieces when people yell at her." She paused. "Where did Brad go?"

"He slipped out the back way and took Cricket with him."

"Why would he do that?"

"Don't ask me why Brad does any of the things he does," said Tracy. "You're his best friend. You know him so well, *you* tell *me*."

"I can't tell you anything until I know what's been going on," Jamie said, pulling a chair out from the table and taking her seat across from Tracy. "All I know is Brad told me he was going fishing, and then he seems to have ended up in Texas. I can see why he might have gone there, but I can't figure out how you fit into the picture."

"I fit into it because he pulled me into it," said Tracy. "Brad came over to the high school and picked me out of the lineup of available accomplices. I don't know why I was the one he zeroed in on, but he gave me a sob story about how he was searching for his long-lost sister, and I was stupid enough to fall for it."

"Well, maybe you'd better fill me in," said Jamie. "I don't even know how he found out Gavin was in Texas. The way Brad feels about his stepfather, Mrs. Brummer didn't want him to know where Gavin was."

"Okay, I'll tell you everything I know," said Tracy. She drew a long breath and forced herself to begin. "Last Tuesday, while I was eating lunch in the school cafeteria . . ."

She meant to make the telling short, but it turned out to take far longer than she had anticipated, because Jamie kept breaking in with questions and comments.

"Gavin stopped taking care of his car after Mindy died," she said, when Tracy mentioned the condition of the Jaguar. "Until then, that bullet on wheels was his pride and joy. After Mindy was killed, he didn't seem to care about the car any longer—or about anything else, for that matter. He just wanted to get away and start life over where everything he saw wouldn't stir up memories."

She reacted again when Tracy described her first glimpse of Cricket seated at the dinner table in the Carvers' kitchen. "It figures that the kid would be blue-eyed and blond," she said. "Gavin has blond hair and blue eyes, so I guess his sister, Cricket's mother, does too. Mindy and Cricket were first cousins. I can see how it might have confused Brad to see a look-alike kid at the table, especially if he'd convinced himself Mindy was at the Carvers'."

"The windowpane was warped," Tracy said, remembering. "Everything we saw through it seemed to be distorted. When Gavin was lifting Cricket out of her high chair, I actually thought for a moment I saw him crying."

"Maybe you did," said Jamie. "Cricket probably reminds him of his daughter. Gavin has plenty of faults, but he did love that baby. He was a good father to Mindy—at least, he tried to be."

"That's not what Brad told me," said Tracy. She regarded the other girl skeptically. "In fact, he said Gavin was so uncaring and irresponsible he burned the little girl with a soldering iron."

"He did," Jamie said, "but that was more my fault than his. Gavin didn't know Mindy was anywhere around."

"It was *your* fault!" Tracy exclaimed. "How could it have been? Wasn't Gavin the one who was holding the iron?"

"I guess Brad didn't tell you," said Jamie. "I was supposed to be watching Mindy. Brad was off camping that weekend, and his mother had gone out shopping, and since Gavin wanted to spend the afternoon working on his car, I volunteered to baby-sit. I got caught up in watching a movie on television and didn't keep an eye on the kid the way I should have. All of a sudden, I heard the screen door slam, and before I could jump up from the sofa, Mindy started screaming. She must have caught sight of her dad and raced straight over to him. By the time he knew she was out there, it was too late."

"That's not the way Brad described what happened," said Tracy.

"Brad wasn't there to see it."

"Didn't anybody tell him?"

"Of course we told him," Jamie said impatiently. "Haven't you caught on yet to how it is with Brad? When you tell him things he doesn't want to hear, he tunes them out. He couldn't bear to believe I was responsible for Mindy's being burned, so he switched things around in his head so all the blame was on Gavin.

"Well, go ahead. What happened after that? How did the two of you get into the Carvers' house?"

"I got a job as Cricket's sitter," said Tracy. "Brad waited outside in the car . . ." She picked up the story at the point at which she had left off and continued until she brought it at last to its painful final chapter. "After we'd crossed the border into New Mexico, I heard a news report about us on the car radio. The announcer said the little girl Brad had told me was Mindy was really the Carvers' three-year-old daughter, Julianne."

By the time Tracy had finished, Jamie's eyes were glistening with tears.

"Poor Brad," she murmured.

"Poor Brad!" Tracy echoed, outraged. "Am I supposed to feel sorry for him? All 'poor Brad' has done since I met him is lie to me and use me. I can't imagine why anybody would do something this bizarre. Why would he pretend Cricket was Mindy? What did he hope to gain? It doesn't make sense."

"He wasn't pretending," said Jamie. "Brad never consciously lies. He gets things twisted up in his mind, that's all. He's never been able to accept the fact that Mindy was dead. The way the accident happened was too awful. He's kept trying to make himself believe that something else happened to her—that she's been stolen away by the bad guys, that one day she's going to come back." She paused. "Has he talked to you at all about his father?"

"He said they used to have good times together."

"Brad worshipped his dad," Jamie said. "Mr. Johnson was an outdoorsy, he-man type. He never should have married the woman he did. He and Brad's mother didn't have a thing in common. He was always off doing his own macho thing in the woods, while she sat at home and made a big show of how miserable she was. If he hadn't made her a widow, I bet that marriage of theirs would have ended in divorce."

"Did Brad know that?" Tracy asked her in surprise.

"He did at the time, but he's managed to forget it. In the years since his dad died, he's shoved the bad memories out of his mind. That's one reason he got so upset when his mother remarried. The man she picked wasn't anything like Brad's father."

"You're making Brad sound pretty creepy," said Tracy. "I thought you said you were his closest friend."

"I am," said Jamie, "but that doesn't mean I don't know he's got problems. After all, I've known Brad for a lot of years. He and I first met back in grade school, when we were nine years old. He was little—and I mean *little*. Much smaller than I was. And he had this sweet face and big brown eyes with long lashes. Another thing different about him was he never wore jeans. His mother thought little boys looked cute in short pants.

"You know how cruel children can be to anybody who stands out from the crowd. There's always one poor kid they all gang up on. Well, that year Brad lucked out. He was the chosen one. The girls made fun of him because he was short, and the boys wouldn't let him into the gang because he was 'pretty.' They called him 'Bradina,' because they said he looked like a girl. He spent every recess sitting by himself at the top of the monkey bars because there wasn't anybody who would play with him."

"How did you get to be his friend?" Tracy asked her.

"Mainly, I guess, because I was different also. I had three older brothers and was kind of a tomboy. I was tall for my age and strong and very athletic. Even the class bullies knew better than to mess with me. I never could stand to see people hurt other people, so at first I stood up for Brad because I was sorry for him. Then later it was because I got to like him. I guess I was lonely too. I needed a friend."

"Has he always been treated badly at school?" asked Tracy.

"No, it was just that one year, until he got his growth spurt. By that time, though, he and I were such close friends that neither of us had much need for other people. Also, Brad was having problems at home, and I was the only one he felt he could discuss them with."

"What was happening to him at home?"

"His folks weren't getting along, and he was caught in the middle," said Jamie. "He couldn't seem to please one without upsetting the other. He never felt totally right about anything he did; either his father was irritated or his mother was crying.

"It finally got so he learned how to split himself in half. He'd say whatever it took to please whichever one of his parents he was with. He'd go hunting with his dad, for instance, and have a terrific time, and then when he got back with his mom, he'd act like his dad had forced him to go and the trip had been boring."

"In other words," said Tracy, "he taught himself to lie."

"I don't consider that lying," Jamie said defensively. "Lying is when you deliberately make things up. I guess I'd call what Brad does 'wishful thinking.' He doesn't tell lies; he believes everything he says."

"Did he invent the fact that his father died?"

"Of course not," said Jamie. "Brad's a little mixed up, but he isn't *nuts*. It happened when he and his dad were up in the mountains. Brad's mother had thrown a fit about their going. It was Brad's birthday, and she wanted him to spend it at home.

"It was while they were up there that Mr. Johnson had his heart attack. Brad had to hike all the way down to the village to get help. By the time he got hold of the forest rangers and they drove back up in a pickup, his dad was dead. Brad's mother fell all apart when she heard the news. She kept screaming at Brad that if he hadn't agreed to go up there, his father would have stayed home and he wouldn't have died."

"He could have had a heart attack at home just as well."

"Her point was that if that had happened they could have gotten him to a hospital. Even when she doesn't make sense, she can be convincing. She spent the next six months in a sanitarium. Brad felt he was responsible for putting her there. He's been scared ever since that she might have another breakdown. He's so overloaded with guilt he can hardly stagger."

"You called him 'a little mixed up,' " Tracy said sarcastically. "It sounds to me like he's a lot more disturbed than that. To convince himself that a strange little girl is his sister—"

"It's his way of keeping himself from cracking," said Jamie. "My mom thinks Brad ought to have professional counseling. I didn't used to agree, but now I guess I have to."

"What if he doesn't go back to Albuquerque?" asked Tracy. "I thought that's where he and Cricket and I were headed, but the fact that he's taken off on his own like this makes it look like he's changed his mind and gone somewhere else."

"Where else *could* he go? He's got that little kid with him. You can't drag a three-year-old all around the country."

"Does he have any relatives besides his mother?"

"An aunt and some cousins up north somewhere, but he hardly knows them. He and I have had our own private buddy system going for so many years that Brad doesn't have anybody else he's close to."

The two girls sat in silence for several moments.

Tracy tried to recall the exact conversation she and Brad had held in the car. The only place he had talked about then was Albuquerque, a "city in a bowl that's surrounded by mountains." She had told him about New York—the high buildings, going to museums with her mother, going to Central Park with her father. He had responded by telling her about the forests and mountains of New Mexico that were "more beautiful than anything you could ever imagine."

"That cabin in the mountains!" she said suddenly. "Do you think that might be where Brad has taken Cricket?"

"Of course!" exclaimed Jamie. "Why didn't I think of that! Brad always takes off for the cabin when things pile up on him."

"Do you know where it is?" Tracy asked her.

"I've only been up there once. My folks didn't go for the idea of Brad and me spending the night there together, and it was hardly worth the trip to go up for just a day. Even so, I bet I could find it if we drove there. It was eight or so miles north of Terrero, on the bank of a stream."

The waitress who had brought Tracy her coffee and sweet rolls materialized behind Jamie's chair.

"Would you like to order, miss?"

"No, thanks," said Jamie. "We're going to have to be leaving."

"Your boyfriend never did come back for you, did he?" the waitress asked Tracy.

"It looks like I've been ditched," Tracy told her wryly.

"Men! I'll tell you, you can't depend on a one of them!" the girl said. "At least it's good your sister could come and get you."

"My sister?" Tracy repeated.

"Aren't you girls sisters? I was sure you were, you look so much alike."

"We're not sisters," said Jamie, staring across at Tracy. "I can see, though, how you might have thought we were. We're the same height and build, and we both wear our hair pulled back from our faces."

"And your eyes," the waitress added. "You've got the same eyes."

Tracy nodded. "I guess that answers my question."

"What question?" asked Jamie.

"Why I was the one Brad chose to be his accomplice."

Chapter 17

Ever since he had pulled off the freeway, Brad had been feeling light-headed and exuberant, as though a tremendous weight had been lifted from his shoulders. It was always that way when he came into the last lap of the journey to the cabin. The vast spaciousness of the landscape between Albuquerque and Santa Fe and the stretches of empty desert that had bordered the highway for miles were now behind him, and he was surrounded by the lush greenery of mountain forestland.

He relaxed in his seat and breathed deeply, greedily inhaling the tangy aroma of pine sap and the clear, clean scent of rushing water in turbulent streams.

He could not believe it had taken him so long to realize that this was where he had to come. If he'd had any sense, he would have planned this from the beginning. It had been a mistake, he now realized, ever even to have entertained the thought of permitting Tracy to accompany them on their flight from Winfield. She should have been left there to deal with the consequences of her own stupid actions. If she had not delayed their leave-taking with her stubborn insistence upon packing up Mindy's clothing, he and his sister would have been safely out of the Carver house long before Mindy's uncle returned for his forgotten theater tickets.

Tracy the Traitor! What had caused her to turn against him? He had placed his faith in her, and she had proved herself unworthy. He had been stunned to emerge from the café dining room to see her standing at the pay phone out in the entrance hall. Her back had been to him, and he could not hear what she was saying, but he had known at once that she had to be turning them in either to the Carvers back in Winfield or to the Rock Springs police.

He should never have asked her to help him in the first place. Still, at the time there had seemed to be no alternative. If Jamie had been willing to come with him, it would have been different. Together, he and Jamie could accomplish anything. He still had not figured out what had happened to Jamie to have made her so reluctant to help him find Mindy. "You don't know what you're doing," she had snapped at him, as though what he was proposing was the scheme of a madman.

Well, Jamie would soon have to acknowledge how wrong she had been. He had managed to accomplish what she had termed impossible. The question now was when and how he should contact her. His plan had changed considerably since leaving Winfield, and he was no longer contemplating a quick return to Albuquerque. His thought now was just to pack in at the cabin for a while and allow himself time to become reacquainted with Mindy. Then, when he was ready, he would drive down to the base of the mountain and use a telephone at the village to get in touch with Jamie.

He would offer her the chance to drive up to join them, but only if she told nobody where she was going. A vision sprang into his mind of himself and Jamie at the cabin, not just vacationing, but living there on a permanent basis. He pictured himself standing out by the stream in the first iridescent light of dawn, wearing his father's boots and waders. He could hear himself shouting, as his father had so often shouted, "Get up, you lazy kid! We've got trout for breakfast!"

He envisioned Jamie, plodding groggily out of the bedroom and then coming to life when she saw the number of fish on his line. Mindy would be with her, rubbing the sleep from her eyes, with one cheek pinker than the other from the pressure of her pillow. He would start coffee brewing and put the fish on to fry, while Jamie got Mindy dressed and combed the snarls from her hair. After breakfast they might go for a hike in the woods or take a walk through the field out in front of the cabin. He could see himself and Jamie strolling hand in hand through the meadow while Mindy bounded ahead, chasing clouds of white butterflies.

The more he thought about it, the more appealing the prospect seemed—he, Jamie, and Mindy, a unit all to themselves. They could do whatever they wanted without interference. No one would even know where the three of them were.

Not even his mother. His initial plan had been to bring Mindy home to her, but he was beginning to realize she did not deserve such a present. It was he who had had to do everything to locate Mindy. His mother had been unsupportive, uncooperative and uncaring in a way that was strange and unnatural in a loving woman. Was it Jamie or Tracy who had asked him, "Doesn't she want her daughter found?" At the time he had instinctively jumped to her defense. Now, however, he had to admit the question was well-founded. If his mother had truly cared about getting Mindy back, she would have made some effort to aid him in his search for her.

He turned his head now to glance across at his sister.

"How are you doing, Mindy baby?" he asked her.

Mindy sat huddled on the far side of the seat with her thumb in her mouth.

"Cricket wants breffuss." The pathetic half whisper was muffled by her hand.

"I know you want breakfast," Brad said. "There hasn't been a restaurant to stop at."

"The Froot Loop place," the child countered.

"I explained to you about that place. The food there wasn't good. It would have made us sick."

"It had Froot Loops!" Mindy protested.

"But they were *bad* Froot Loops. They would have given you a tummy ache."

"Where's Tracy?" Mindy asked him. "Cricket wants Tracy."

"Tracy was busy on the telephone. She couldn't come with us."

"I want Mommy," the little girl said, and began to whimper.

"Now, don't start that crying again," Brad told her, struggling to be patient. "I didn't have breakfast either, and I'm as hungry as you are. In fact, I'm going to stop right now and get us some food. Around that bend in the road up ahead there's a little store. We'll stop there and load up on groceries, and I'll be sure to get Froot Loops."

The store was the same one he had had in mind as a logical place to be calling from when he had phoned the Hansons from Winfield and said he was in the Pecos. Stopping there now, he first filled the car at the self-serve pump in front of the store, and then, leaving Mindy curled up in the front seat to wait for him, he went inside to pay for the gas and purchase supplies.

"Brad! Hey, boy, how's it going?" The man behind the counter greeted him warmly. "Long time, no see! I've been wondering if you were going to come up this spring."

"Hi, Renzo! Good to see you! You're looking great," Brad said. "Are the trout really biting like it says in the newspapers?"

"They'll tear the hook off the line," Renzo said with a chuckle. "Oh, on the subject of things you read in the papers . . ." His voice lost its effervescence and became low and somber. "Back last fall, I read about your family tragedy. I sure am sorry about what happened to your sister. I meant to send you and your ma a card, but time got away from me, and I didn't get it done."

"That's okay," Brad said. "It was rough for a while, but it's over now. We've got her back, and in the long run, that's all that matters."

The man stared at him blankly.

"You've—*got her back?!*"

"She's outside in the car right now," Brad told him. "I need to stock up on stuff for us to take to the cabin. It seems the kid's turned into a sugared-cereal freak. You wouldn't happen to have any Froot Loops, would you?"

"Sure," Renzo said slowly. "I got all sorts of sugared cereal. That's all anybody who comes up here ever asks for. It's on the shelf at the back right next to the Pop-Tarts." He paused. "Now, run this past me again. You say you've got your sister *back?*"

"She's right out there in the car," Brad repeated.

"In that blue Chevy parked out there by the gas pump?"

"That's a pretty safe bet, considering it's the only car in the lot."

While Renzo turned to stare out the window, Brad took a basket from the rack by the door and went to the back of the store to load it with groceries. As he did so, he ran through a mental list of the foods Mindy liked. Puddings in cans with pop-up lids. Cocoa with marshmallows. Hot dogs and dill pickles. A jar of spaghetti and meatballs. Ruffles potato chips.

After he had his basket filled with supplies, he carried it to the front of the store and set it down on the counter.

"So, how many sisters you got, Brad?" Renzo asked a bit too casually as he totaled up the bill.

"Only one," Brad said.

"She younger or older than the one who got hit by the car?"

Brad regarded the man in bewilderment.

"I said, I only have one sister. All I've ever had is one sister. You can look out the window and see her there in the front seat."

"I already saw the kid in the car," said Renzo. "I guess I must be mixed up about what happened. It was some-body else who got killed, then, is that it? That newspaper story was wrong? It was another kid?"

"I don't know what you read in the paper," said Brad. "But as you can see, my sister's doing just fine. I'm taking her up to the cabin to teach her to fish."

He paid for the groceries, noting as he did so that he was running low on cash. When he phoned Jamie, he would have to ask her to bring up some money.

He went back out to the car, opened the rear door, and set the bags of groceries on the back seat. Then he climbed into the front and started the engine. Mindy was still in the same position in which he had left her. Her thumb was in her mouth, and her free arm was locked around the toy monkey.

"That thumb-sucking business has got to go," Brad said. "Is that something you started doing in Texas?"

The child regarded him solemnly and did not answer.

"I'm asking you a question, Mindy," Brad said.

"Cricket," the little girl murmured without removing the thumb from her mouth.

"Mindy," Brad said. "Your name is *Mindy*, not Cricket. I can see where Jamie and I have our work cut out for us."

He pulled out of the parking lot and turned east onto the road leading up from Terrero into the hills. The fact that this weekend was the culmination of spring break in the public schools was evidenced by the number of families who had come up to the mountains to wind up their children's week-long holiday. In the camping area just beyond the village, pickup trucks, mobile homes, and campers were parked bumper to bumper. Any space that remained was jammed with pup tents and deck chairs, and the air was thick with smoke from charcoal grills. The blast of conflicting rock music played at top volume on an assortment of portable ghetto blasters all but drowned out the shrieks and laughter of romping children.

Beyond this, the road rose abruptly into the forest, looping back and forth in a series of hairpin curves. Steep and winding, it required skillful driving to maneuver, but each twist and turn revealed a spectacular new vista as pine woods gave way to groves of shimmering aspen and green meadows became frosted over with blue and yellow wildflowers. In one spot, a stand of silver birch trees stood out from the surrounding greenery, smooth and tapered as candles, and in another, a galloping stream hurled itself dramatically over the edge of a suicidal drop, only to resume its journey more placidly a hundred yards below.

As Brad took the car around a curve, a deer leapt out in front of him, so close that its feathered tail brushed against a fender, and farther on, a raccoon strolled casually along by the side of the road as though expecting the driver of some passing vehicle to stop and offer it a lift.

The dirt road leading to the cabin wound off into the trees just short of the access point to the footpaths and horse trails that led into the depths of the wilderness area. When he turned here, Brad had to shift down into first gear. The snows of the previous winter had engraved deep ruts in the hard packed earth, which spring rains had then filled with water, and the Chevy lurched and slid and floundered in mud as it inched its uncertain way forward and upward. Bushes scraped and slapped at the sides of the car, and branches clawed at the windows with sharp, taloned fingers, as though they were trying to force their way in through the glass.

Mindy covered her face with her hands and wailed.

"I told you, no more crying," Brad reminded her.

"Don't like it here," sobbed Mindy. "Cricket wants to go home!"

"We *are* nearly home," Brad told her. "It's not much farther. Once we hole up in the cabin we're going to be safe."

But was that true? The question occurred to him suddenly. To whom had Tracy been making her surreptitious phone call? In the car after leaving Winfield, he had talked so much about the cabin that she might suspect that he would take his sister there. Of course, she did not know its exact location, but anyone who stopped in the village could find that out from Renzo.

What if Tracy had decided Mindy belonged with the Carvers? What if she had called the police to report that Brad had taken her? Although Gavin did not have legal claim to the child, neither did Brad. It was his mother who had been awarded custody, and at the time, she had seemed to want it very much. Still, once the legal battle was over, as Tracy's father had demonstrated, the responsibility of full-time parenting could seem less appealing. The fact that their mother had shown so little interest in getting Mindy back did seem to indicate that she was no longer eager to raise her. If the police should arrive at the cabin and confiscate the child, it was not inconceivable she might be returned to Gavin.

Well, he would not allow that to happen, Brad vowed silently, glancing across at the girl on the seat beside him. He had not brought her this far to give her up now. No one was going to take Mindy, as long as he was able to prevent it, and he had no intention of leaving her unguarded.

The road was becoming steeper and more rutted the farther they progressed. After about three quarters of a mile, they came to a rise, and the Chevy lunged up it, grasped, lost its grip, and slid back down. Brad floored the accelerator, and the car shot forward again for a second charge. This time its tires caught hold and it managed to haul itself laboriously upward until it reached the peak of the slope and plunged triumphantly out into the knee-deep grasses of a mountain meadow. Brad put the car into neutral and switched off the engine.

Immediately the world was filled with the trill of birds and the far, sweet song of wind in rustling branches.

"There it is," Brad told Mindy reverently. "Look up there!"

The cabin was nestled in a hollow on the lower slope of a hill, like a small brown wren settled snugly into a nest. The mountain cedar grew so thick around it that the trees seemed to be holding the little house in their arms, and the stream that tumbled by at the base of the porch was a leaping, laughing miracle of churning silver.

Brad opened the door of the car and got out.

"Come on, Mindy," he said. "We can't drive any closer than this. We're going to have to walk across the field and climb that hill. We'll take just enough supplies right now so we can eat and get ourselves settled, and I'll come back later and bring up everything else."

He opened the rear door and extracted the groceries.

Mindy shook her head stubbornly and refused to look at him. "Don't like it here," she muttered. "Want to go home."

"You can take Monk-Monk with you," Brad said enticingly. "There's nothing to be afraid of. I'm here to take care of you. If anyone comes, we'll hear their car when they're a long way off. Nobody's going to take you away from me, baby." He shifted the sack of groceries into the crook of his left arm.

Then, with his free right hand, he picked up the gun.

Chapter 18

It was mid afternoon by the time they reached the Pecos, and later still when Jamie finally maneuvered her car up the last steep stretch of muddy road that brought them over the top of the rise and out onto the grassy plateau across from the cabin.

She pulled the car to a stop next to Brad's and shut off the motor.

"So, he's really here," Tracy said, gazing across at the familiar blue Chevy that stood opposite them.

"The man at the store in the village told us he would be."

"I know, but I still can't believe we ever found this place." Tracy gave the field a hasty perusal. "Where's the cabin?"

"Up there," Jamie said, gesturing toward the hill on the far side of the meadow. "It's hard to make out anything with the sun in your eyes. It's in all that foliage by the side of the stream."

"Oh, I see it now," Tracy said, squinting into the blinding glare of the afternoon light. "I can see why Brad had to park the car down here. There's no way anybody could get a vehicle up between those trees."

"This is backpacking country," said Jamie. "We're

right at the edge of the Wilderness. It's lucky for us there was a road that came in this far."

She opened the door on her side of the car and climbed out. Shading her eyes with her hand, she stared up at the shadows that encompassed the cabin.

"I think there's somebody out on the porch," she said.

"Is it Brad," Tracy asked, "or Cricket?"

"I can't tell. I just thought I saw some movement there by the steps." Jamie drew a long breath. "Brad, is that you?" she called.

There was a moment of silence; then Brad's voice floated down to them.

"How did you get here, Tracy? Where did you get the car?"

"He thinks you're me!" exclaimed Tracy, making an automatic move to open the door on the passenger side.

"No, stay where you are," Jamie cautioned. "It's better if he keeps thinking he's dealing with only one of us." Raising her voice again, she called to the boy on the hill above her, "This isn't Tracy, Brad! It's Jamie!"

"Get back!" Brad shouted. "You can't fool me, Tracy Lloyd! I know why you're here! You want to take Mindy back to Gavin! Well, I'm not going to let you have her! You know I've got a gun!"

"You're faking, Brad!" Jamie took an impulsive step out into the field. "You don't have a gun, but even if you did, you'd never shoot anybody!"

"Don't bait him like that!" hissed Tracy. "He does have a rifle. He used it to threaten Doug Carver. Face it, Jamie, Brad's as dangerous as he is crazy!"

"Don't you *dare* call Brad crazy!" Jamie said angrily.

"What term would *you* use for someone who threatens to kill people?"

"He's been pretending too long, that's all," said Jamie. "You don't have any idea of all that Brad's been through. It's enough to have made anybody act sort of—different."

"Tragedies occur, and people live through them," said Tracy. "Brad's not the only person in the world to lose someone he loved."

"With him it's worse than just having lost his sister."

"You mean, there's more to the story?"

"Yes, there's more."

"I don't understand. What else could there possibly be?"

"I don't want to talk about it," Jamie said shortly. "None of it would have happened if his mother hadn't pushed him so far."

"I don't think this is something we ought to be dealing with," Tracy told her. "I think we should go back to Terrero and call the state police."

"No," Jamie objected. "We just can't do that to Brad. This whole stupid thing would get blown out of all proportion. I'm going to go up there and try to talk some sense into him. No matter how upset and confused he is, he'd never hurt *me.*"

"Look, we're not the only two people involved here," said Tracy. "Maybe you're right, maybe you could march straight up there and nothing bad would happen to you. But the thing is, Cricket's in that cabin too. If Brad should go nuts with that gun, anything could happen. We can't afford to take chances with a little girl's life."

"All right," Jamie said. "First, we'll get the Carver kid out. After that, I'll go up and see if I can reason with Brad."

Tracy regarded her doubtfully.

"You actually think he'll allow Cricket to come down here?"

"No, of course he won't, but one of us can go up and get her. Brad knows I'm here, but he hasn't caught a glimpse of you yet. He doesn't have any idea there are two of us. The door on the passenger side faces away from the cabin. If I divert his attention by walking out into the middle of the meadow, you can jump out of the car and make a dash for the trees."

"What, then?" Tracy asked skeptically. "What good would that do?"

"Once you're in among the cedars, you'll be as good as invisible. You can work your way around the edge of the meadow to the base of the hill. There's a path that starts over there by that big clump of bushes. It runs along the side of the stream, all the way up through the woods. If you take that, it will lead you to the back door of the cabin."

"Then what would I do?" Tracy asked her. "Open it and walk in? I don't think Brad's going to have the welcome mat out for me."

"He'll be out on the steps, just the way he is now," said Jamie. "He can't see what's happening inside when he's busy talking to me. You can slip in through the back, grab Cricket, and get her out of there. It shouldn't take you more than a couple of minutes."

"That might work," Tracy conceded, "provided the back door's unlocked and Cricket's in the house and not out front with Brad. Let's say I do get her out, though, what happens after that? When he discovers what we've done, won't he take it out on *you*?"

"Brad would never do anything to hurt me," Jamie said confidently. "Well, what do you say? Are you game to give this a try?"

"It doesn't look like I have any choice," said Tracy.

"No, you don't," agreed Jamie. "Not as long as I hold the car keys. There's no way you can get back to Terrero unless I drive you."

In the short time the girls had been talking, the sun

had dropped lower in the sky, and it was now balanced precariously on the peak of the hill. Its rays were suddenly filtering through leafy branches, and the vibrant green of the meadow had become more muted, as though it were being viewed through a pair of tinted sunglasses. A breeze moved across the field and the long grass came to life, bending and rising and bending again in a fluctuating wave. As Tracy sat watching Jamie move slowly out into the midst of the turbulence, she had the strange impression the girl was entering an ocean.

"What do you think you're doing now?" Brad shouted.

"I want to get out where you can see me!" Jamie called back to him. "Look at me, Brad! You've got to see that I'm Jamie! I've come here because I want you to go back home with me!"

How confident she sounded, how sure of her place in his life!

Well, I wasn't in love with him anyway, Tracy tried to tell herself.

Not "in love," perhaps, and yet, he had kindled something—a spark of light in the depths of her inner darkness. She had thought she could never feel anything again for anybody. Now she realized she *could,* but she still wasn't sure why she would want to.

She waited until the other girl had reached the center of the meadow before she made her move. Then she quietly opened the door and slipped out of the car. Jamie had parked just past the top of the rise, so it was only a matter of yards to the edge of the woods. Tracy covered that distance quickly, keeping in a direct line with the car so it would cut off any view of her from the cabin.

Once safely concealed by the trees, she breathed a sigh of relief—and then discovered she was in for more problems. The undergrowth was thicker than she had imagined, and forcing her way through it was a marathon battle. Low-hanging branches whipped across her face, and bramble bushes ripped and tore at her clothing. By the time she had finally reached the foot of the hill, her cheeks were raw and stinging, and her arms and legs were covered with cuts and scratches.

As Jamie had predicted, a space between the bushes at that spot opened onto a narrow trail that led up through the trees. As Tracy began to ascend it, the sound of rushing water, which until then had been no more than a background whisper, became increasingly louder. When the path took a sudden sharp turn to the right, she abruptly found herself on the brink of the stream.

From there on, the trail became nothing more than a narrow catwalk along the bank. Water tumbled past, swirling around rocks and churning in unseen basins, and Tracy's shoes were soon soaked from the leaping spray. The roar of the stream obliterated the sound of Brad's and Jamie's voices, and the woods and the water became a world of their own. The one connection with reality that made it possible for her to continue to relate to the situation that had brought her there was the sight of two sets of footprints imbedded in the soft, damp earth—the deep impression of Brad's leather loafers and the smaller, slighter indentation made by Cricket's tennis shoes.

Although the trail was not particularly steep this low on the hill, Tracy found that the unaccustomed altitude made even an easy climb difficult. It was only minutes before she was gasping for air and her heart was pounding. Then, just when she had decided she could go no farther without a rest stop, she glanced up and saw the roof of a small log house jutting out from beneath a canopy of leaves. Several yards ahead of her the path she was on veered away from the stream and led directly up to the cabin's back door.

She was close enough now to hear Brad's voice from the porch at the front of the house, no longer raised in anger, but lower and much more calm. When she strained to listen, she thought she could hear a girl's voice also, although the words being spoken were impossible to make out. She wondered if Jamie had climbed the hill from the front and if she and Brad were now standing together on the steps. If this was the case, she hoped that Cricket was not with them, or if she was, that Jamie would find some pretext for sending her back into the house.

Breathing more easily now that she had had a moment to recuperate, Tracy resumed her trip up the path to the rear of the cabin. Two slabs of flat rock had been placed one on top of the other to form steps leading up to the back door. She tried the knob and was relieved to feel it turn in her hand. She gave the door a shove and it swung open, revealing a narrow, rectangular room laid out in two sections. The front portion obviously served as a living room, for it was furnished with a high-backed couch and two overstuffed chairs. The back section contained a table, four straight-backed chairs and a wood-burning stove.

Cautiously, after a moment's hesitation, Tracy stepped in through the doorway. The door at the front of the house stood open also, and she could hear Brad's voice clearly, along with the lighter tones of Jamie's voice. Although their voices did not sound angry, they were obviously arguing.

". . . know you can't stay here long," Jamie was saying. "It was one thing, baching it here by yourself or with your dad, but a little kid can't be expected to rough it, with no indoor plumbing or anything."

"Mindy'll love it here, once she gets used to it," Brad insisted. "She got fussy this afternoon because she needed a nap."

There was only one door off of the kitchen area. It was closed, and Tracy assumed it must lead to a bedroom. Moving as silently as she could, she tiptoed across the kitchen, cringing as a board creaked under her feet and maneuvering around haphazardly placed chairs. Turning the knob of the door, she pushed it open. The small bedroom that lay beyond contained only two bunk beds and a chest of drawers.

Cricket was lying on one of the bunks, but she was not sleeping. Her eyes were open, staring up at the ceiling, and her face was puffy and red and streaked with tears. Her breath was coming in little gasping hiccups, as though she had cried herself into a state of exhaustion. In her arms, she cradled the shabby toy monkey.

"Cricket?" Tracy said softly. "Cricket, it's me."

The child evidently had not been aware that the door had been opened, for she gave a start and jerked her head around to stare at Tracy.

Her eyes showed first fear and then recognition. "He said you wasn't coming!" she exclaimed.

"Shh," Tracy warned in a whisper, raising her finger to her lips. "Be very quiet. We don't want anybody to hear us." She crossed the room to the bed and bent to gather the little girl into her arms. "We're going to sneak out the back, and then we're going home."

Releasing her hold on the monkey, Cricket clasped both arms around Tracy's neck

"To Mommy?" she asked hopefully in a tiny voice.

"Yes, to Mommy," Tracy promised, keeping her own voice low. "And, boy, I bet your mommy will be glad to see you!"

She lifted the child from the bed and, holding her tightly in her arms, carried her back out through the door to the kitchen. The conversation at the front of the house was still going on. Brad was saying, "You will too, if you give it a chance here."

"He's bad," Cricket whispered, tightening her grasp on Tracy's neck. "That boy's bad. He's got a gun to shoot people!"

"He's not going to shoot *us*," Tracy told her reassuringly. "We're leaving this place right now, and we're not coming back."

She crossed the kitchen with slow, careful steps, avoiding contact with furniture, awkward and thrown off balance by the child she was carrying. She was attempting to transfer the full weight of her burden to her left arm so as to free her right hand to open the door when Cricket startled her by suddenly saying, "No!"

"Shh!" Tracy cautioned her. "We'll talk when we get outside."

"No!" Cricket said again, more loudly. "No! Wait! Where's Monk-Monk?"

"He's back in the bedroom. We can't get him now. We'll come back for him later."

"No! Monk-Monk! I want Monk-Monk!"

Releasing her hold, Cricket shoved both hands hard against Tracy's chest. The child was surprisingly strong for someone so little, and Tracy felt her one-armed grip beginning to loosen.

"Cricket, stop this!" she whispered frantically. "That monkey's just a toy! You can get a brand new Monk-Monk when you get home."

"No!" cried Cricket, giving a violent lurch.

The weight of the struggling child was more than she could handle. To keep from having to drop her, Tracy bent and set her down. The moment her feet touched the floor, Cricket broke free and took off at a run in the direction of the bedroom.

Frozen in helpless horror, Tracy could see what was going to happen a split second before it did.

The sound of the little girl colliding with a chair was followed almost instantaneously by the roar of a gun.

Chapter 19

Afterward, Brad could offer no explanation for the shooting. His last clear memory before the gun discharged was of standing with Jamie on the tiny front porch of the cabin, looking down into her face and thinking how beautiful she was.

It was strange he had not noticed that before. Perhaps it was because she had become so familiar. For him, looking at Jamie was like gazing at a painting that had been hanging at the center of his life for so many years he had stopped taking in the richness of its colors.

He had chosen Tracy to help him because she had reminded him of Jamie. But no one could take Jamie's place—not now, not ever.

How could he have failed to recognize her, even at a distance? It had been the car that had confused him. He was accustomed to seeing Jamie behind the wheel of the Hanson family station wagon and had forgotten about the secondhand Charger in their garage. Jamie had bought it for next to nothing through an ad in the newspaper and had been tinkering with it for months, trying to get it running. Now she had accomplished that, as she eventually accomplished everything she set out to do. *Deter-*

mined, clear-eyed, practical—those were the words he had always connected with Jamie.

And now he had another adjective—*beautiful.*

That realization had struck him with startling clarity while he stood watching her climb toward him up the face of the hill. Her face had been awash with gold from the slanting afternoon sunlight, and the radiance of the vision had set fire to his heart.

She had been flushed and winded when she finally reached him and stood, panting, at the edge of the porch, hanging onto one of the posts like a child swinging on a maypole while she struggled to catch her breath.

"Hey, that's quite a climb! That hill is steeper than it looks!"

"You could have gone around back and come up the trail," Brad said.

"It would have taken too long." She attempted a smile, but it stopped at her lips and was not reflected in her eyes. "It's pretty grotesque being greeted by a guy with a gun. What are you doing with that? Are you planning to shoot me?"

"Don't be silly. It's for—well, it's for . . . *protection.*" Brad let the muzzle drop so the rifle was pointed at the floor. "I'm glad you came. I've been *hoping* you'd come. I've missed you."

"I've missed you too," said Jamie. "It's been a long week."

"I've got a surprise for you. Guess who's up here with me? Guess who's in the bedroom of the cabin right now?" Brad reached out a hand and lightly touched her cheek. It was a gesture he had never thought to make before, and he was startled by the softness of her skin. "It's Mindy! I found her in Texas where Gavin was hiding her! I was thinking maybe the three of us could stay here all summer."

"That's a nice idea," Jamie said, "but it couldn't work. It's pretty up here, of course, but you know you can't stay here long. It was one thing, baching it here by yourself or with your dad, but a little kid can't be expected to rough it, with no indoor plumbing or anything."

It was a down-to-earth argument, as all her arguments were. Jamie never angered him the way other people did. So if he wasn't angry, how had the thing come to happen? One moment, he had been standing there with his back to the open door, the rifle held loosely in one hand with its muzzle aiming downward. Then, there had been a crash, and he had spun to face the cabin, automatically jerking the gun into a raised position.

Somehow, it had gone off.

For several moments after the blast, Brad stood unmoving, cemented in place, too stunned to react at all. Then, as the significance of what had occurred penetrated his consciousness, he let the rifle fall and dashed into the house.

The scene that greeted his eyes was not unexpected. It had been hidden at the back of his brain for four terrible months, held at bay like pain held back by a local anesthetic, waiting for the inevitable moment when numbness would subside. The golden-haired child on the ground, a woman's figure bent over her—the meaning of the tableau came rushing in upon him, and he could no longer refuse to acknowledge its validity.

The protective wall of denial began to crumble, and as the bricks fell away, there was nothing left but reality.

"I did it," Brad said quietly. "I killed Mindy."

The terrible words that slid from his lips so softly, expanded upon their release to fill the room like thunder. *I did it. I killed Mindy*—Mindy—MINDY! They bounced back at him from walls and floor and ceiling, reverberating from every part of his being.

The world began to spin, and his legs buckled under him. Sinking to his knees, he covered his face with his hands, and against the blackness he again saw the setting. The yard in front of their house had clumps of brown grass sticking through an anemic layer of half melted snow. Gavin's Jaguar stood out by the curb, highly polished and perfect. His own car, the blue Chevy, was parked in the driveway.

It was winter. It was December.

It was Mindy's second birthday.

Gavin had arrived at noon to attend the celebration.

"This is crazy!" Brad told his mother. "This guy's not your husband! You've divorced the creep, so why is he hanging around here?"

"It's Saturday," his mother reminded him. "You know Gavin gets visitation on the weekends. I'd rather put up with him here at Mindy's party than have them go off and celebrate her birthday without me."

The accusation hung, unvoiced, in the air between them.

"Dad would have had the heart attack anyway," Brad said defensively, feeling his stomach tighten with old, familiar nausea.

"We can't know that," said his mother.

"The doctors told us—"

"He lay in the woods for three hours without medical attention. If the two of you had stayed here at home as I begged you to, we could have summoned an ambulance in a matter of minutes." She sighed. "Well, it's behind us now. What's done is done. The men in my life may desert me, but I'll always have my children."

To Brad's relief, she did not pursue the subject further.

Mindy was still too little to understand why the day was so special, but she reveled in her position as center of attention. The house was filled with a combination of Christmas and birthday decorations; a tree with lights and tinsel, mistletoe hanging over the doorway, multicolored balloons, and a birthday cake with two legitimate candles and a third one "to grow on" set off to the side.

The birthday presents were wrapped in pastel paper to distinguish them from the Christmas gifts under the tree. There were a Raggedy Ann, a jack-in-the-box, a xylophone (Brad had gotten her that), and a dollhouse half a foot taller than Mindy herself.

What Brad had not been prepared for was the bear.

Until that appeared, he had prided himself on the fact that he was managing to keep his animosity under wraps. For his mother's sake and Mindy's, he had made an effort to be congenial, making casual conversation, dishing out ice cream to serve to the four of them, answering Gavin's awkward questions about how school was going.

But when Gavin was ready to leave, he had insisted they all walk out to the car with him, and from the back seat he had lifted a big, soft package. He had presented it to Mindy with a dramatic flourish, and a brown toy bear had emerged from the fluff of pink paper.

That was the point at which Brad's self-control deserted him.

"Mindy already *has* a bear!" he exploded. "In case you've forgotten, I gave her Bimbo a year ago today!"

"This isn't just *any* old teddy bear," Gavin assured them. "Pinch him, Mindy baby, and see what he does."

Mindy glanced uncertainly from her brother to her father. Then she reached out tentatively and touched the bear's paw.

Gavin guided her hand to the furry arm.

"Give him a squeeze!" he said, and Mindy giggled.

With Gavin's hand over hers, she squeezed the bear's arm, and from somewhere deep in its chest a hidden music box began to play "Deck the Halls With Boughs of Holly."

Mindy let out a shriek of surprise and grabbed the bear with both hands to pinch it again. Immediately, the tune it played changed to "Jingle Bells."

The little girl threw her arms around her father's neck.

" 'Dinkle Bells'!" she squealed in delight. " 'Dinkle Bells'!"

"He plays twenty different songs," Gavin informed her proudly, as self-satisfied as though he had programmed the creature himself. "I guess this beats old Bimbo, doesn't it, baby?"

Those were the words that had opened the emotional floodgate. The rage that had swept over Brad was so all-consuming that it had been all he could do to keep from striking the man. If he had been more heavily built he might actually have done so, but knowing he was no physical match for his former stepfather, he had stood in wretched silence, shaking with unconsummated fury, his fists clenched so tightly his fingernails sliced into his palms.

Exactly what happened next, he had never been sure about. He did recall the fact that the phone had rung inside the house and his mother had left the yard to go in to answer it. The stupid bear was now playing "Silent Night," and Gavin was going through the ritualistic good-byes with hugs and kisses for Mindy and a token handshake for Brad.

Brad had glared at the man and turned away, unable to bring himself to take the proffered hand. Instead, he had jumped into the Chevy and started the engine. Gunning the motor, he had thrown the car into reverse, and a moment later had been flying down the road to Jamie's.

Had there been a thump as the car roared out of the

driveway? When he thought back now, he knew of course that there had been. At the time, he had been too furious to focus on anything but his anger, and he had driven away without a glance behind him.

Now, in the terrible blackness of his two cupped hands, he saw the nightmare through from beginning to end.

"It was an accident," he whispered. "I didn't mean to. Mom says it's the same as murder, but it was an *accident!*"

"Of course it was an accident," Jamie said softly. "That's why you weren't indicted; it was an accident."

The pain of the realization was so intolerable that Brad did not think he had the strength to survive it.

"I killed my sister," he moaned, "and I can't bear it."

"Yes, you can," Jamie told him, "because I'll bear it with you."

Her hands seized his and pulled them down from his face, forcing him to look straight into her eyes. When he did, he saw his agony reflected there and knew she had taken half of it for her own.

She put her arms around him and drew him against her, so the curve of her breast was a pillow for his face. The tears came then, in a rush that almost drowned him, and with the storm of weeping, the great release.

"Why is that boy in there crying?" asked Cricket.

"He was scared," Tracy told her. "When that gun went off by accident, he thought the bullet hit you and knocked you down."

"My foot got caught on the chair when I ran for Monk-Monk."

"I know, but Brad was outside and couldn't see that. He thought he'd hurt you, and that made him feel just awful."

She and the child were walking together along the

bank of the stream below the cabin. The sun had now slipped behind the hill, creating an artificial twilight in which nothing appeared to be exactly what it had been. The meadow beneath them was lost in mysterious shadows, a fairyland or a breeding place for devils. The stream could have been a gush of blue-black liquid from a witch's cauldron or a mirror reflecting the high, sweet curve of heaven.

It's however I choose to see it, Tracy thought suddenly, as she gazed at the painful but glorious world that surrounded her.

"Are we going home now?" asked Cricket, tugging at her hand.

How strange that the word brought with it a vision of Winfield!

"Yes," Tracy told her quietly, "we're going home."

About the Author

LOIS DUNCAN is the author of over thirty best-selling books for young readers and adults. Among her most popular suspense novels for young adults are *Locked in Time* and *The Third Eye* (Junior Literary Guild selections); and *Stranger With My Face, Killing Mr. Griffin,* and *Summer of Fear* (ALA Best Books for Young Adults); all available in Dell Laurel-Leaf editions. *The Twisted Window* is her first novel for Delacorte Press.

Lois Duncan and her family live in Albuquerque, New Mexico.